Happy Birthday Harlequin
25 Successful Years!
Hope there are many more.
Best Wishes
Anne Mather

Dear Reader,

Welcome to the twenty-fifth anniversary of Harlequin Presents®—a perfect opportunity for opening a bottle of champagne and toasting the world's most exciting romance line.

I've had the privilege of contributing to it for over twenty happy, fulfilling years, and I can't imagine a better job.

I love to read as well as write, and I've been fascinated to see how Presents has developed over the years to meet the romantic needs and aspirations of so many women. Long may it continue.

With love,

Sara Craven

Sara Craven

SARA CRAVEN

Ultimate Temptation

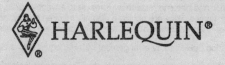

TORONTO • NEW YORK • LONDON
AMSTERDAM • PARIS • SYDNEY • HAMBURG
STOCKHOLM • ATHENS • TOKYO • MILAN • MADRID
PRAGUE • WARSAW • BUDAPEST • AUCKLAND

ISBN 0-373-11963-1

ULTIMATE TEMPTATION

First North American Publication 1998.

Copyright © 1997 by Sara Craven.

All characters in this book have no existence outside the imagination of the author and have no relation whatsoever to anyone bearing the same name or names. They are not even distantly inspired by any individual known or unknown to the author, and all incidents are pure invention.

This edition published by arrangement with Harlequin Books S.A.

Printed in U.S.A.

CHAPTER ONE

'LUCY—check out the guy on the end table. Have you ever seen anything so gorgeous?'

Lucy Winters felt herself shrivel inwardly as Nina's penetrating stage whisper reached her ears—and, presumably, those of everyone else around them at the pavement café. She stared down at the guide to Tuscany she was studying, wishing she could climb inside it, closing the covers behind her.

Her only hope was that this unknown Adonis was either stone-deaf or spoke no English. But one swift, embarrassed glance in his direction told her instantly that her optimism was unfounded.

She saw a profile that Michelangelo might have sculpted in bronze, etched now with lines of total disdain. A high-bridged, aristocratic nose complemented a firm mouth, curling in contempt and annoyance, and a strong chin jutted arrogantly as their owner signalled to the waiter for his bill. He turned to pick up a flat leather briefcase from the adjoining chair, and for a moment his eyes, cold as frozen amber, met Lucy's.

They said that ice could burn. And Lucy felt as if she'd been scorched from head to foot.

She muttered urgently, 'Nina—for heaven's sake. He heard you.'

'Well, what of it?' Nina was unrepentant. 'That's what these Italian studs live for—being looked at—admired. There he goes.' She leaned back in her chair, sighing gustily. 'God, look at the way he moves his hips. I bet he's a sensation in the sack.'

5

Lucy, wincing at her companion's crudity, watched the tall figure's retreat with more clinical interest.

Yes, he was almost classically good-looking, although his thick, waving black hair was worn rather too long for her taste, she decided with detachment. And he moved with a careless grace which was probably instinctive rather than studied. But he'd clearly resented being the object of Nina's blatant interest, and made no bones about it either. And who could blame him?

Not, Lucy thought, a man to cross.

She said drily, 'I think there could be more to him than that. He was wearing a designer suit—probably Armani.'

Nina giggled. 'I was more interested in what was underneath it,' she returned, unabashed. 'I'm beginning to like Italy.'

She signalled to the waiter to bring two more cappuccinos, and Lucy returned to her guidebook.

Not for the first time in the forty-eight hours since their arrival, she found herself wondering if she'd done the right thing.

It had been a total shot in the dark, agreeing to share a villa in Tuscany with three other girls who were comparative strangers to her. But she'd been desperate to get away—to have a break—a complete change of scene.

And when she'd heard Nina, who worked in the accounts department, lamenting the fact that the fourth member of their projected house party had let them down virtually at the last minute, she'd heard herself, to her own astonishment, saying, 'I'll go with you.'

Three weeks of Tuscan sun would have been unthinkable while she was with Philip. He liked action holidays—white-water rafting, orienteering in Scotland, rock-climbing in Wales—and Lucy had masked her apprehension and tried to join in. Flotilla sailing in the Greek islands had been the nearest thing to relaxation he would agree to, but Lucy had turned out to be not a very good sailor.

Maybe his open irritation and impatience with her during that last trip should have alerted her to the fact that all was not well with their relationship. Or maybe love really did make you blind, after all, she thought, trying not to look at the pale band on her finger where his ring had been.

When he'd told her, quite abruptly, that there was someone else, she'd been devastated. But, looking back, she realised the signs had been there for a while.

She'd watched numbly while he briskly packed his things, and moved out of the flat they'd been sharing. Hers, of course, to begin with, but that was through choice. Now she had to choose again—to decide whether to stay there with all her memories or find somewhere new.

'You can always camp out with us for a while,' her sister Jan had told her, her pretty face wrinkled with concern. 'Until you find your feet.'

Lucy loved Jan, and her enormous rugby-playing brother-in-law, and her pair of permanently mud-stained nephews, but she'd known that moving in with them all, however temporarily, was not the answer.

'That's one of the reasons I'm taking this holiday—to think—to get my life sorted.' She'd tried to smile. 'It takes time to adjust.'

'But is this the right way to do it?' Jan sprinkled sugar over the fruit in the pastry case in front of her. 'Sharing a house with a girl you hardly know, and two of her friends?' She shook her head. 'Sounds like a recipe for disaster to me.'

'Well, you stick to apple pies.' Lucy tried to sound cheerful. 'I've seen a photograph of the Villa Dante and it looks fantastic, besides being absurdly cheap. It belongs to a friend of the manager of the Italian restaurant that Sandie and Fee go to after their language class.'

'Not a proper holiday company?' Jan's frown deepened, and Lucy hugged her.

'Stop being a mother hen. It'll be marvellous. I might even get some painting done.'

'Well, if you're sure.' Jan sighed. 'Oh, damn Philip. I can't believe he's done this to you.' She paused, giving Lucy a wary glance. 'Who is this new lady?' she asked carefully. 'Do you know?'

Lucy ate a slice of apple to cover her grimace. 'Remember he changed his job a few months ago—went to a merchant bank in the City? Apparently she's the chairman's daughter.' She added stonily, 'He always was very ambitious.'

'That's not the word I'd choose,' Jan said grimly. 'Well, you forget about the two-timing swine and have a great holiday.'

That had been Lucy's intention, but she'd been conscious of her misgivings even on the flight to Pisa, when the others had taken full advantage of the free drinks offered by the stewardesses, as well as engaging in a noisy and uninhibited flirtation with a group of young men across the aisle.

Lucy, staying off alcohol because it had occurred to her that someone had to drive the rented car awaiting them at Pisa, had seen some of the scathing looks directed towards them by other passengers. She'd also been aware that some of the men opposite had girls with them who were beginning to look downright hostile.

But her attempt to cool the situation had been treated with derision by her companions.

'What a drag,' she'd heard Sandie mutter to Fee. 'No wonder her boyfriend dumped her.'

Tommaso, their landlord, had been waiting at the airport with the car—a smart little Fiat—and the keys to the villa. He was younger than Lucy had expected, efficient and more than charming, but she hadn't warmed to him.

And one glance from his bold dark eyes had told her that neither her slender shape, her smoothly bobbed hair nor her wide, faintly slanting hazel eyes held the least appeal for him. Her companions, in their skimpy sundresses, high on booze and excitement, were far more to his taste, and he'd ogled them shamelessly while conducting the necessary negotiations.

Lucy had not expected to hand over her share of the rental in cash, there and then, but the others had seen nothing wrong in it, so she'd supposed she was being overly fussy.

'Isn't there an inventory we should see?' she asked doubtfully, but Tommaso waved that away with one of his wide smiles.

'Any problem—you tell the maid, Maddalena,' he decreed.

'And if she can't deal with it?' Lucy's voice was cool. She'd come to Italy to relax, but this was altogether too casual.

Tommaso shrugged. 'Then you come to me.' He gave her a dog-eared card with a hand-written address on it. 'I live here, in Montiverno.'

Lucy, struggling to accustom herself to the left-hand drive, as well as the unfamiliar clutch, felt consumed by pessimism about the whole enterprise, especially when her merry companions insisted she make a detour so that they could glimpse the famous Leaning Tower before they left Pisa.

'Bloody thing looks straight,' was Nina's slurred comment from the back seat.

Lucy sighed under her breath as she edged carefully out of Pisa and headed south.

It was a wonderful day, the sun warm in a faultlessly blue sky, the faint breeze redolent of pine and rosemary. She found herself driving past fields of sunflowers, through tiny villages bright with flowers and shuttered against the heat, and always on the edge of her vision were the untamed rolling hills. The others had fallen asleep, so Lucy had it all to herself, and was content.

Following the sketch map Tommaso had given her, she bypassed Montiverno—a small town clinging to its rocky hilltop, and dominated by a ruined fortress—and turned into a wide valley lined by terraces of vines and silvery olive groves.

And, as she rounded a sharp bend, there, somewhat to her surprise, was the Villa Dante, its name carved into one of the tall stone pillars which flanked the gateway.

An imposing entrance for a holiday let, Lucy thought as she steered the Fiat carefully through the high wrought-iron gates and up the long, winding drive where cypresses stood like dark sentinels.

And when the house came finally into view, standing proudly back from a broad gravel sweep, Lucy felt the breath catch in her throat.

It was love at first sight.

She braked gently and sat, drinking in ancient walls the colour of pale apricot, the faded terracotta roof, the wide stone steps leading up to the heavily timbered front door.

The photographs in London hadn't done it any kind of justice, she thought almost reverently. It was like some exquisite antique painting set in the matchless frame of the golden Tuscan landscape.

'Well, it'll do,' Fee remarked as she emerged from the Fiat. 'I hope to God the plumbing works.'

Maddalena was waiting to greet them. She was small, her black hair was liberally streaked with grey, and she was patently nervous. She barely spoke or smiled as she led them on a swift tour of inspection.

The villa had been built on three sides of a large courtyard, surrounded by a colonnaded veranda, with the usual shady loggia on the first floor. In the centre of the courtyard was a large stone fountain into which water poured eternally from a tilted urn upheld by a smiling nymph, while steps led down to a broad terrace with a swimming pool, and finally to a tumble of garden with tall hedges, gravelled paths and banks of roses and flowering shrubs running riot beyond.

Inside, the rooms were spacious, and while not over-furnished they gave the impression that each item had been selected with great care.

Lucy's eyes widened as she assimilated the dining room, with its frescoed walls, massive polished dining table set off by ornately carved wooden candelabra and tall-backed formal chairs, and then went into the formal *salotto*, with its exquisite ceiling, elaborately patterned in coloured plaster, the wide stone fireplace, big enough to roast one of the wild boar for which the region was famous, and the cavernous but supremely comfortable leather sofas.

All this grandeur for the kind of rent we're paying? Lucy questioned silently, but the others seemed to take it in their stride.

'A bedroom each, and a couple over,' Nina exulted. 'Let's hope we get lucky.'

Lucy was hoping for nothing of the sort. That kind of encounter had never been her style, and she felt too raw and vulnerable to contemplate even the most casual of relationships.

The first couple of days passed tranquilly enough. They sunned themselves, bathed in the pool and enjoyed Maddalena's excellent cooking. Sandie and Fee spent a fair amount of time on the telephone, having low-voiced giggly conversations.

Lucy could only pray they weren't calling home to Britain, or the bill at the end of their stay would be horrendous, and her funds were strictly limited.

But she would worry about that when the time came. In the meantime, she could revel in the drowsy ambience of her surroundings, and the unusual luxury of having a maid to wait on them.

Except, this morning, Maddalena hadn't turned up.

'Perhaps it's her day off,' Nina commented crossly as she wrestled with the coffee-machine. 'Did she say anything to you, Lucy?'

'She hardly says anything at all,' Lucy admitted wryly. 'She still seems scared to death of us.' She looked at Sandie. 'Why don't you go down to her cottage and see if she's all right?'

'Why me?' Sandie bridled.

'Because you and Fee have been to Italian classes,' Lucy reminded her patiently.

Fee pulled a face. 'And a lot of good it's done us so far. But I'll try and get some sense out of her,' she added, with the air of one making a great concession.

She was back almost at once. 'There's no one there,' she reported. 'I had a look through one of the windows and the place looks deserted, as if she's cleared out altogether.'

'Oh, Lord.' Nina was alarmed. 'Our money—our travellers' cheques...'

But all their personal possessions and valuables were still safely in place.

'She must have got fed up with the job,' Fee said discontentedly. 'But maid servce is included in the price Tommaso's charged, so he can bloody well provide someone else. We'll tell him after we've been to the *alimentari* this morning.'

Which was how Lucy now found herself sitting in Montiverno's main square drinking coffee with Nina, while the other two shopped for provisions—something they'd volunteered to do, to her surprise.

They came back laden, and smiling like cats with a saucer of cream.

'You'll never guess who we bumped into in the supermarket,' Sandie said airily as she sat down. 'Those guys we met on the flight over—Ben and Dave. Ben's parents have got a summer place just a couple of miles away at Lussione. Isn't that an amazing coincidence?'

Her face and voice were equally guileless, but Lucy spotted the wink she directed at Nina.

They'd clearly been in touch with each other from the start. That was what all the phone calls were about, she thought resignedly. And this morning's shopping trip had been a rendezvous.

'So tonight we're throwing a little party—a welcome to Tuscany bash for us all. They thought it was a great idea.' Fee adjusted her sunglasses nonchalantly.

Lucy stared at her. 'You're having this party at the villa?'

'Why not?' Sandie challenged.

They were all glaring at her suddenly, looking as if they were waiting for her to put a damper on everything. As she felt she must.

'It doesn't seem the right setting for that kind of thing.' She felt about one hundred and three. 'A lot of the furniture's old and very valuable. And Tommaso may not want a lot of strangers on his property.'

'Well, if you're so uptight about it, ask him,' Nina flung at her. 'Get his permission at the same time you tell him about Maddalena. Ask him to join us, if he fancies it.' She looked at her watch. 'I'm going to look in that little boutique down the road. We'll see you back here in an hour.'

Now I really am the outsider, Lucy thought as she climbed up through the maze of narrow cobbled streets towards the *rocca*. Party pooper par excellence.

She stopped to check the address Tommaso had given her, frowning slightly. She'd asked for directions at the café before setting off, but the houses in this area seemed far too shabby and run-down for the man who controlled the Villa Dante. The paint was peeling off many of them, and the roofs needed attention as well, their tiles either slipping or missing altogether.

A scrawny dog, lying in a patch of shade, lifted its head and growled at her as she went past, peering at the numbers on the doors.

Tommaso's house was in the middle of the street. Two cracked steps led to the front door, and a broken shutter hung at a crazy angle from the main ground-floor window.

When the bell didn't work, Lucy hammered on the door, but to no avail. There was no sound or movement in the house.

She stood on tiptoe, peering through the window. The room was totally bare. No furniture. No sign of life at all.

Lucy bit her lip as she stepped back onto the street. First Maddalena, she thought uneasily, now Tommaso. What on earth's going on?

She glanced round, uncertain what to do next. Her phrasebook didn't equip her to deal with errant maids and missing landlords, and she had the uncanny feeling, anyway, that she was being watched from several adjoining houses, and not in any kindly spirit either.

I'd better find the others—tell them, she decided, and began to retrace her steps, glad to get away from the mean, narrow street and its unseen eyes.

But she must have taken a wrong turning, because she found herself in a different square altogether. No bars or bustle but dominated by an elaborate Gothic church, and completely deserted apart from the statutory pigeons.

Lucy heard her own footsteps echoing as she crossed the cobbles and she paused, wondering which of the many alleys leading off the square would take her back to the town centre.

The silence was oppressive—threatening. Then suddenly it was shattered by the roar of a motorcycle coming from behind her.

The pigeons flew up in a flurry of alarmed wings. Lucy spun round, had a confused impression of two figures, leather-clad and anonymous in helmets, and realised a gauntleted hand was reaching towards her as the bike swerved in her direction.

She cried out, and tried to jump back as the hand snatched at the strap of her shoulder bag and tried to jerk it from her. But Lucy clung on grimly, refusing to let go. She heard the snarl of the throttle, warning her that the bike was about to accelerate away, and was pulled forward, falling painfully onto the cobbles. She was going to be dragged behind the bike if she didn't release her bag.

She screamed, 'No,' her voice cracking, half in fear, half in anger. Then she cried, 'Help me, someone,' and heard a man's voice shout in answer.

She saw a dark figure running towards her, felt another shoulder-wrenching jerk at her bag, and then suddenly the metal clips on the strap gave up the struggle and she was left lying on the ground, winded, bruised but free, her bag still clutched in both hands, while her assailants sped off with the dangling strap as their only prize.

It seemed safer to stay where she was. Her heart was pounding, she was shaking all over, and she felt deathly sick. She was dimly aware of someone bending over her, of a man's deep voice speaking urgently in Italian, of a hand touching her shoulder.

'No.' She was galvanised into panicky reaction, kicking out. 'Get away from me.'

She heard him mutter something under his breath as her foot connected with his shin. He said curtly in English, 'Don't be a fool, *signorina*. You called out for help. Can't you see that's what I'm trying to do? Are you badly hurt? Can you sit up?'

Wincing, Lucy allowed him to help her into a sitting position. The hands that touched her were gentle as well as strong, and a faint musky scent of masculine cologne teased her senses.

She turned her head slowly and looked at him, tensing with dismay as she realised that her saviour was none other than the man from the pavement café.

Nina's designer stud, she groaned inwardly. It would be.

At close quarters, he was even more devastating. Handsome as a Renaissance prince, and, she acknowledged as his eyes narrowed in recognition, just as distant.

'So, we meet again,' he commented without pleasure. 'What are you doing, wandering alone like this? Don't you know it isn't safe?'

'I know now.' She lifted her chin and gave him her own brand of dirty look. 'Actually I was looking for someone, and I thought things like this only happened in big cities.'

'Unfortunately, criminal elements from bigger places now sense there's a living to be made even in towns like Montiverno.' His tone was dry. 'Now, let's see if you can stand.'

She would have dearly loved to slap his patronising hand away, not to mention his sneering face, but she let him help her to her feet. She was bitterly aware that she was filthy from her contact with the ground, and that her new white cotton trousers were torn beyond repair. Every part of her seemed to be throbbing, and she knew an ignominious impulse to burst into tears.

Instead, she said, her voice wobbling slightly, 'They wanted my bag, but I wouldn't let them have it.'

'*Stupida!*' he said crushingly. 'Better to lose your bag than be killed or maimed.'

Lucy pushed her dishevelled hair out of her eyes with a shaking hand. She said, 'I've just been through one of the worst experiences of my life, and all you can do is criticise.'

'No,' he said. 'That's not all I can do. My car is nearby. I will drive you to the clinic for a check-up.'

'No.' The denial was instinctive and immediate, driven by some deep female consciousness that motorbike thieves were far from the only danger in the situation.

He was very still, his brows rising in regal hauteur. He said very quietly but with cool, relentless emphasis, 'I beg your pardon?'

To add to her other ills, Lucy felt herself blushing all over as the amber eyes swept over her, slowly and comprehensively.

She said hurriedly, 'I mean—thank you, but there's no need for you to bother any more. I'm fine—really. Just—a little shaken.'

'And prey, I think, to certain illusions.' He was smiling, but there was no amusement in his eyes. 'I am offering my help, *signorina*, but nothing more. I do not require sexual favours as a reward for my assistance, whatever fantasies you or your friend may enjoy,' he added bitingly.

The contempt in his face and voice stung Lucy like a flick from a whip. There was no real reason to feel so mortified, she told herself angrily. He was a stranger to her, and she was never going to see him again, so what did it matter if he thought she was tarred with the same brush as Nina?

Yet somehow, and quite ridiculously, it seemed to matter a lot.

She said stonily, 'Think what you wish, *signore*. I'm grateful for your help but not your opinion of me.'

'Then accept my aid,' he said. 'Believe that I cannot simply walk away and leave you here like this.' And, when she still hesitated, he added, 'But on the other hand, *signorina*, I do not have the entire day to devote to your interests either. So please make up your mind.'

Lucy bit her lip. 'Well—perhaps a lift back to the main square. I'm meeting my friends there.'

'Of course,' he said softly. 'No doubt there will be more male talent to be reviewed. You should take care, *signorina*. You are not in the cold Anglo-Saxon north now. To provoke a Tuscan is to play with fire.'

She gave him a frigid Anglo-Saxon look. 'Please don't worry about me, *signore*. I'm fireproof, I assure you.'

Not that she felt it. Her abiding impression was that she had been run over by a bus, but she gritted her teeth and limped along beside him to where his car was parked in an adjoining street.

It was a sports car, naturally, black, long and low, with concealed power in every menacing line. Rather like its owner, Lucy decided, trying to extract some humour from the situation and signally failing.

She accepted his assistance into the passenger seat with as much dignity as she could muster, and sat in silence, hoping she was not bleeding onto his upholstery, as he expertly wove his way through the tangle of streets and traffic, out into the bustling familiarity of the main square again. Where he halted.

He said with cool politeness, 'You are sure I may not take you to the clinic?'

'Absolutely. The damage is only superficial, and I had an anti-tetanus jab before I came away.' Lucy was aware that she was babbling, and stopped. 'You've been very...' She halted again. The only word she could think of was 'kind', so she said it, although she wasn't convinced it was appropriate.

She fumbled for the door-catch, and he leaned across her to release it. Again she was aware of that tantalising musky fragrance, and of the disturbing warmth of his body close to hers. Too warm. Too close.

She met his gaze, saw a tiny flame dancing in the amber eyes, and heard herself swallow. Deafeningly.

He said sardonically, 'So you think you're fireproof?'

He leaned forward, took Lucy's chin in his fingertips and kissed her on the mouth, slowly and very thoroughly.

Then he released her, and, with a graceful wave of his hand, indicated that she was free to go.

Burning, Lucy stumbled out of the car. Only to hear his voice following her, softly, mockingly.

'I hope your Italian stud did not disappoint you. *Arrivederci, signorina.*'

Then, silently as a panther, the car slid away, and she was left staring after it, a hand pressed to her trembling lips.

CHAPTER TWO

FOR heaven's sake, Lucy castigated herself wearily, not for the first time. You're not a child. You've been in love with a man. You've lived with him. So one kiss, even from a complete stranger, is no big deal. Pull yourself together.

She was lying on the bed in her room at the villa, staring at the ceiling. Trying to get all that had happened into some kind of perspective.

The others had been genuinely shocked and concerned when they'd returned from their boutique trip and found out what had happened to her. At first, they'd wanted to call the police, but Lucy had vetoed this. She had neither the number of the motorcycle nor any adequate description of its riders. Besides, apart from the ruin of her bag and trousers, she'd lost nothing, and her only witness had driven off into oblivion.

She'd described him solely as a passer-by. It seemed wiser not to revive Nina's interest, or lay herself open to any inconvenient questions, she'd decided, passing the tip of her tongue over her still tingling lips.

Nina had driven the Fiat back to the Villa Dante with exaggerated care, while Sandie and Fee had plied Lucy with offers of everything from grappa to a homely cup of tea.

They'd been frankly sceptical, however, when she'd told them about Tommaso. The collective feeling was that she'd gone to the wrong address.

'I mean, would a man who owns a place like this be camping out in some kind of slum?' Nina had demanded, and Lucy had to admit it seemed unlikely.

Tomorrow, she'd thought, she would make proper enquiries.

However, there was still no sign of Maddalena, which meant Nina and the others had to prepare for their party themselves.

Lucy, however, was not expected to help. Nina had escorted her somewhat perfunctorily upstairs, asked if she wanted anything, and vanished at Lucy's polite negative.

Once alone, she'd filled the big sunken tub which took pride of place in the adjoining bathroom, and soaked herself luxuriously, letting the warm water soothe as well as cleanse.

She had superficial grazing on her knees and elbows, and there would undoubtedly be bruising to follow, but she would survive, she'd decided with a faint sigh.

But her injured feelings were not as easily mollified, she'd thought as she'd dried herself carefully and put on her lemon silk robe.

It was galling to be classified with the man-hungry Nina, but probably unavoidable under the circumstances. However, she would never have to face her tormentor again, so the only sensible course was to put the whole basically trivial incident behind her, and enjoy the rest of her holiday.

Hers was not the largest bedroom, but it had the best view across the valley, and she liked the uncluttered lines of its furnishings and the plain, heavy cream drapes. It occurred to her now that the room was almost masculine in concept. Maybe this was where Tommaso usually slept, she thought, her flesh creeping at the very idea.

Someone had brought up a pitcher of fruit juice and some paracetemol while she was in the bath. It was a genuinely kind thought, and maybe it would mark a new phase in her somewhat chequered relationship with her companions.

They were younger than her, even if it was only by a matter of a few months, perfectly aware of their own considerable attractions, and looking for a good time. And where was the real harm in all that?

You should stop being so critical and join in more, she told herself forcefully. Make the best of things, starting with tonight's party. Remember that you're single too now, instead of half of a couple.

Aided by the painkillers, she slept for a while, her dreams confused and disturbing. And, throughout them all, a man's dark figure walked on the edge of her consciousness, his face as proud and beautiful as a fallen angel's.

She awoke in the twilight with a start, her hands reaching across the empty bed for a presence that didn't exist, and lay still, waiting for the drumming of her pulses to subside.

Philip, she thought. I must be missing Philip.

She did not feel particularly rested, and she was beginning to stiffen up, too, her bruises announcing their existence. It wouldn't have taken much for her to cry off from the evening's festivities and stay in her room, she acknowledged, hauling herself gingerly off the bed and over to the big, heavily carved *guardaroba*. But then solitude had no particular appeal either. It gave her imagination too much scope, she decided wryly.

Most of the clothing she'd brought with her was casual, but at the last moment she'd thrown in a dress that was strictly after-dark gear.

She looked at it without enthusiasm. Philip had urged her to buy it, against her better judgement, during the last week they'd been together. It wasn't her style, being brief-skirted and body-hugging, with the neckline slashed, back and front, to a deep V, which did no favours at all for her slender curves. And that shade of dark red was wrong for her too, draining her own natural colour.

It seemed to have been designed for a very different woman, and having caught a brief, piercing glimpse of Philip emerging from a fashionable Knightsbridge restaurant with his new lady—a vivid brunette built on voluptuous lines—she could guess only too well who'd he'd been thinking of when he'd picked it out.

But it was the only party wear she had, she thought as she zipped herself into it. And maybe it would do her good to wear it, as a tangible reminder of how little her relationship with Philip had come to mean.

She had spent days and nights since their break-up tormenting herself with self-blame. Asking how she could have been so blind, or why she hadn't suspected in time to put things right—win him back.

Now, as she brushed her hair into a smooth curve swinging just above her shoulders, she knew there was nothing she could have done. And found herself questioning for the first time whether she should even have tried.

For the truth was, she realised almost dispassionately, that the magic had gone out of their lives long before he'd left.

In the first, euphoric flush of love, she'd ignored the fact that their lovemaking fell short of rapture for her. That Philip had always seemed more concerned for his own satisfaction than hers. That, invariably, she was left stranded, aching for a fulfilment which she could only guess at, having never actually experienced it in reality. And, towards the end, it had become perfunctory—almost a mechanical ritual because they shared a bed.

But how was it that she could suddenly see all this so clearly? she wondered, biting her lip in confusion.

Because today a man had kissed her—someone she would never meet again—and in those few moments when his mouth had possessed hers she had been shaken to the depths of her being, her body shocked into an instant arousal she had never known before.

In her dreams, it was not Philip she had sensed at all, but this other man—the warmth of his breath on her cheek, the scent of his skin, the casual strength of the arms which held her. And in her dreams she had wanted more—much more—than his kiss alone.

She looked at herself, half-wonderingly, in the mirror, her hand going once more to her lips.

She thought, Dear God, what's happening to me? And could find no answer in her heart.

In spite of all her good resolutions, Lucy could not get into the swing of the party.

The guests had arrived, already uproarious, bringing a crate of assorted wine and a ghetto blaster blaring out heavy rock.

Fee had prepared an enormous bowl of spaghetti carbonara, which they ate in the dining room. Lucy winced as she saw Dave carelessly stub out his cigarette on the corner of the huge polished table.

'What a fabulous place,' Ben commented, leaning back in his chair. 'You were damned lucky to find anywhere in this neck of the woods. When my parents first came out here looking for a holiday place, they found everything in the district belonged to a crowd called Falcone—bankers from Florence, by all accounts. And they weren't prepared to part with one inch of land, or a single brick of property.'

'Falcone?' Lucy questioned, frowning. 'How strange. There's a carving of a bird like a falcon over the main door here. I wonder if there's a connection?'

'Lucy,' Fee said patronisingly, 'is heavily into old buildings. She notices things like that.'

Hal leaned forward. He was tall and blond, older than the others.

'Maybe she could switch to the present day and notice me instead.'

He gave a mock leer, making everyone laugh, but Lucy noticed how his eyes lingered on her cleavage, and felt uncomfortable.

Ben picked up one of the bottles on the table. 'Or we could all notice this—Chianti Roccanera—one of the Falcone local by-products.' His voice took on a reverent tone. 'Dad would kill me if he knew we'd helped ourselves to some of this.'

Nina raised her glass. 'Then let's drink a toast to Ben's father, and all the Falcones, including the one over the door,' she said lazily. 'And our landlord, Tomasso Moressi, who managed somehow to beat the system.'

When supper was finished, they rolled up the rugs in the *salotto* and danced. Lucy found herself watching the pairing-off process with detached interest. That it was not going to be to everyone's liking was more than evident.

Nina singled out Greg, with whom she'd been flirting on the plane and who was, apparently, unattached, so that was all right. But Ben's girlfriend, Sue, was frankly mutinous watching him gyrate with a laughing Fee. And Sandie was blatantly intent on winning Dave away from Clare.

Aware that Hal was heading in her direction, Lucy decided hastily that she would be better employed in clearing the remains of the meal. The dining room looked as if a bomb had hit it, she thought ruefully as she collected the dirty plates. Food had been spilled. A puddle of wine had collected on the table from an overturned bottle and dripped onto the floor. A lamp on a sidetable had been knocked over and damaged, and one of the beautiful crystal goblets had been smashed.

And the kitchen was even worse. Fee seemed to have used every pan and bowl to concoct her spaghetti. Lucy sighed soundlessly, tucked a towel round her waist, and set to work.

The noise of the party seemed to be receding, and presently she heard splashing and laughter coming from outside. When she went to investigate, she found them all down at the poolside.

It was a warm, sultry night, with the sky blazing with stars. The ornamental lamps had been lit, and someone had changed the cassette for one with music of a slower, dreamier tempo.

Greg and Nina were dancing slowly, as if they were welded together. He was kissing the side of her neck, pushing down the straps of her dress as he did so.

Fee and Sandie were in the water with Ben and Dave, obviously skinny-dipping, their discarded clothing lying in untidy heaps on the tiled surround. Sue's face was frozen as she watched them, and Clare was biting her lip, close to angry tears.

There's going to be trouble, Lucy deduced resignedly. And I don't really want to be involved.

As she turned to go, she found Hal blocking her way.

'Running out on us?'

Lucy lifted her chin. 'I've had a bad day. I think I'll go to bed.'

'What a wonderful idea.' He gave her a slow, meaningful smile. 'I'll keep you company.'

She didn't return the smile. 'I think you'd do better to stay with your friends,' she said evenly. She nodded towards Sue and Clare. 'Some of them don't seem very happy.'

'They can look after themselves,' he dismissed. 'I've been watching you all evening. You're a bit of a dark horse, Lucy.' His eyes slid over her, making her feel as naked as the revellers in the pool. 'So, what's your story?'

She took his hand from her arm. 'I haven't one. And, if you don't mind, I'd like to go.'

'Oh, but I do mind.' His voice hardened slightly. 'Whatever the lads get up to tonight, tomorrow it'll be kiss and make up with Sue and Clare. I've seen it all before. I'm sticking with you. You intrigue me.'

'I'm afraid it isn't mutual.' Lucy's tone was icy. She turned away, seeking another means of retreat, but Hal grabbed her by the shoulders and swung her round to face the others.

'The lady wants to leave,' he announced. 'What do you say?'

'Oh, let her go,' called Fee. 'Winters by name, wintry by nature,' she added with a giggle. 'She's no loss.'

'No, chuck her in here.' Ben's voice was slurred. 'Serve her right for being a spoilsport.'

'But don't ruin her pretty dress,' Greg added, leering, and Nina began to laugh.

'Off, off, off,' she chanted, and the others joined in, only Sue and Clare maintaining a tight-lipped silence.

Lucy froze as she felt Hal's hands, odiously familiar, fumbling for her zip. Felt her dress beginning to slide from her shoulders.

'No.' Frantically, she kicked backwards, her sandal heel connecting smartly with his shin. He swore and his grip slackened fractionally—momentarily.

It was enough. Lucy pulled free and ran round the pool towards the sheltering darkness of the garden, desperation lending her speed, in spite of her aches and pains.

She had some crazy idea of trying to reach the car parked at the side of the house. But there was something blocking her way again. Or someone, her mind registered helplessly as she was captured and held.

Greg must have cut her off. At the very least, she was going to be stripped and thrown into the water, and every fibre of her being recoiled in revulsion from the thought.

'Let me go.' She began to struggle fiercely, punching and clawing at the imprisoning arms. 'I said, leave me be, damn you.'

'*Sta' zitto.*' The low voice was grimly familiar. 'Shut up, you little fool, and be still.'

'You?' Lucy stared up at the dark, patrician face, and her voice cracked with relief, and another, less easily recognisable emotion, as she acknowledged, 'It's you.'

Involuntarily, she found herself pressing against him and burying her face in his chest as she drew a shuddering breath.

For a moment he let her remain where she was, then he put her away from him and walked forward into the lamplight.

All heads had turned towards him as if they were on strings. The laughing and shouting had died away as if a switch had been thrown, to be succeeded by a strangely intense silence into which his voice, quiet and cold, fell like a stone.

He said. 'I am Giulio Falcone. And this is my house. May I know what you are doing here?'

'Your house?' Nina was the first to break the spell his appearance had created. She faced him, flushed, tousled and frankly aggressive. 'What the hell are you talking about?'

'Easy,' Ben intervened sharply. 'It is him. It's Count Falcone himself.'

'I don't care who he is,' Nina flung back. 'This place belongs to Tommaso Moressi, and we're renting it from him.'

'You are mistaken, *signorina*.' Count Falcone's voice was like steel. 'The man you speak of, Moressi, is no more than the nephew of my servant, Maddalena. He owns nothing apart from what he can steal,' he added contemptuously. 'I hope you have not been unwise enough to pay him anything.'

'I'm afraid we have.' Lucy spoke, her voice hollow, her hands shaking as she put her dress to rights. 'Three weeks' rent, plus the use of a car and maid servce. Only the maid has disappeared—and so has Signor Moressi.'

'I don't doubt it.' Giulio Falcone shrugged. 'Almost certainly word of my unexpected return spread at once, and he took fright.' He shook his head, more in sorrow than in anger. 'Poor Maddalena. She has always indulged that worthless fool.'

'Poor Maddalena?' Fee echoed shrilly. 'To hell with that. What about us—our money?'

She had climbed out of the pool, and the Count's face tightened with distaste as he glanced at her.

'Be good enough to cover yourself at once, *signorina*,' he directed with icy formality. 'I regret that you have been the victim of a confidence trick, but that is hardly my problem. What I must demand is that you vacate my house immediately.' He looked around, frowning. 'Are you all staying here?'

'No.' Ben was huddling into his clothes. He looked awkward and faintly ridiculous. 'My parents have a place near Lussione.'

'Then I suggest you return there. And take your friends with you,' Giulio Falcone added bitingly.

'No,' Lucy said forcefully, her shocked negation instantly echoed by Sue and Clare.

'You bring these slags back with us and I walk out.' Sue glared at Ben.

The Count's lip curled. 'We seem to have an impasse,' he drawled. 'I suggest you settle it amongst yourselves before I am forced to call the *polizia*.' He glanced at his watch. 'Shall we say fifteen minutes?'

His mention of the police had an oddly galvanising effect. Within seconds, the poolside was clear and the erstwhile tenants of the Vila Dante were on their way upstairs to pack.

As Lucy passed the door of the *salotto*, she could hear a furious argument going on between Ben and the others. Hal detached himself from it and came to the door.

'It's all right, sweetheart.' His eyes swept over her in an appraisal that combined sensuality with malice. 'You don't have to worry about a thing. I've got my own room at Ben's place. I'll make sure you're looked after—as long as you start being friendlier.'

She said with icy clarity, 'Over my dead body,' and went up to her room, two stairs at a time.

Her heart was thudding like a sledgehammer as she began to empty the chest of drawers and the wardrobe, hardly aware of what she was doing as she tried to think—to plan. She'd have to cut her losses altogether, she told herself as she piled everything untidily into her case. Somehow she'd have to make her way to Pisa and get a flight home. Anything else was unthinkable.

She presumed she'd be able to transfer the return half of her ticket to a different flight. If not, she'd simply have to pay all over again.

I'll worry about that when I get there, she told herself as she dashed into the bathroom to collect her toiletries.

When she returned to the bedroom, she realised with another thump of the heart that she was no longer alone.

Giulio Falcone was lounging in the doorway, watching her.

'You don't have to check up on me,' she said quickly, aware that her breathing had quickened, and resenting the fact. 'I've almost finished.'

'So I see.' He was silent for a moment. 'Are you so eager to go to Lussione?'

'You know I'm not.' She pitched her toilet bag into the case and rammed the lid shut.

'No? You don't want to be with your friends?'

She bit her lip. 'They're not my friends.'

His brows lifted sceptically. 'Yet I observed an unusual level of intimacy for mere acquaintances,' he murmured.

Lucy flushed, remembering exactly what he must have seen. 'They're just some people we met on the plane,' she said. 'Nina and the others wanted to give a party— and invited them here tonight.'

'Yes,' he said with chill emphasis. 'I have seen the trail of destruction they have left—particularly in the dining room.'

'I didn't get around to that,' Lucy admitted wearily. 'But I tidied the kitchen.' She lifted her chin. 'And I'm sure we'll be happy to make good any damage.'

He laughed. 'You are being naïve, *signorina*. Both the lamp and the glass were antiques of great value. Replacement would be impossible, and the cost inestimable.'

Lucy's heart sank. 'Well, we could all chip in,' she returned bravely. 'And, of course, the police may find Tommaso Moressi and get our money back. You could have a claim on that, I suppose.'

'I think Tommaso will be a long way from here by now, with his tracks safely covered,' Giulio Falcone commented drily. 'Leaving his unfortunate aunt, as usual, to pick up the pieces,' he added cuttingly.

Lucy looked down at the floor. 'I understand now why she didn't want us here. She seemed very frightened.'

'I can imagine,' he said sardonically. 'Yet it should have been safe. I had no plans to use the villa myself until the time of the vintage. But circumstances intervened.' He shrugged. 'You are unfortunate, *signorina*. You could so easily have enjoyed your holiday uninterrupted and innocently unaware that your occupation was illegal.'

The last word seemed to hang in the air between them, raising all kinds of disturbing implications.

Lucy shivered. She said, 'I'm not sure enjoyment is the word.'

'No?' The amber eyes surveyed her reflectively. 'Yet you are dressed for an evening of pleasure.'

Lucy gritted her teeth. That damned dress, she thought.

'A bad mistake,' she said. 'Like the entire trip.' She forced a smile. 'And being mugged was really the last straw anyway. I didn't need to be conned as well.'

'How did you meet Moressi—hear about this place?' he asked curiously.

'The others used to visit a pizzeria after their Italian classes. The manager arranged it. He and Tommaso must have been in league with each other.' She was silent for a moment. 'I wasn't sure about him from that first moment in Pisa. And when I saw this house—how beautiful it was, and how old—it seemed even stranger. He didn't—fit somehow.'

'He never has.' His voice was abrupt. There was another silence, then he said, 'So, what is the alternative to Lussione?'

'Pisa,' she said determinedly. 'And the next flight home.'

'That could present problems. This is, after all, the holiday season. There will be few spare seats available— if any,' he added starkly.

Lucy shrugged defensively. 'Then I'll find somewhere to stay—go on stand-by,' she said with more confidence than she actually felt as she did a hasty mental calculation of her available funds.

'Can you affford that?' Clearly he wasn't fooled.

'I don't have a choice.' She gave him a defiant look.

'How fortunate,' he said softly, 'that I was able to read your mind so accurately.'

'What do you mean?' Lucy was suddenly very still.

'Your friends have gone. I told them you would not be accompanying them.'

Lucy stared at him, suddenly, tensely aware of how quiet the house had become.

'You mean they've left me here alone?' Her voice almost cracked. 'Without even a word?'

His smile deepened. There was something pagan in the curve of his mouth, she thought, a stir of unbidden excitement warring with the growing apprehension inside her.

He said gently, 'Not alone, *signorina*. You forget that I shall be here too. From now on you will be staying as my guest.' He paused. 'And also,' he added softly, 'as my companion.'

CHAPTER THREE

LUCY stared at him. She was suddenly aware that she was trembling. That all the warmth seemed to have drained from her body, leaving her ice-cold.

There was danger here, all the more shocking because it was totally unforeseen.

Her hands curled into fists at her sides, her nails grating across the soft palms. She tried to keep her voice level.

'Companion, *signore*? I don't think I understand.'

'It's quite simple. You will remain here, *signorina*, to make reparation for the insult which has been made to my home—my family—by you and your—acquaintances.'

'*I'll* remain?' She took a startled breath. 'But that isn't fair...'

Giulio Falcone shrugged. 'By your own admission you cannot afford proper recompense for the damage that has been done. However, there are other methods of payment.' His smile barely touched the corners of his mouth. 'I believe we can reach a settlement that would be—agreeable to us both.'

'Then you're wrong,' Lucy said furiously. Cold no longer, she was now burning with shame and anger, and an odd sense of disappointment. 'How dare you even suggest such a thing? Who the hell do you think you are—and what do you take me for?'

'I am Falcone.' He threw back his head, the dark face arrogant, brooding. 'And you are a girl who has twice trembled in my arms. Can you deny it?'

'I was upset,' she flung at him defensively. 'The first time I'd nearly been robbed, and the second I was running away. I thought you realised that—and why...'

'Ah, yes.' His voice was reflective. 'But, in that case, why tempt a man by wearing a dress that begs to be taken from your body and then deny him the pleasure? Your companions, after all, showed no such reticence,' he added, his mouth curling slightly.

She said shortly, 'I'm responsible for no one's conduct but my own, and I don't play games like that.'

'Are you a virgin?'

She gasped, the colour deepening to fiery red in her face. 'You have no right to ask me that.'

'A simple "no" would have sufficed,' he said mockingly. 'Although—' he sent her a narrow-eyed glance '—your eyes do not have the look of a woman who has known all the satisfaction that love can bring.'

'I don't know what you're talking about,' Lucy said haughtily.

He laughed. 'I'm quite sure you don't, but it will be an exquisite pleasure to teach you some day—or some night.'

There was a caress in his voice which shivered down Lucy's spine and danced in her pulses. She felt the muscles in her throat tauten.

She managed a brief shrug of her own. 'Fortunately, I shan't be around that long. As I said, I'm leaving for Pisa.'

'Ah,' the count said meditatively. 'And just how do you propose to get there?'

Lucy paused in the act of locking her case. 'Why— drive there, of course.'

'I did not realise you had brought your own vehicle.'

'Well, I haven't, but...' Her voice trailed into silence as she saw his smile deepen mockingly, and the slow negative movement of his dark head.

She said unsteadily, 'Of course, the car is yours too. I should have realised.'

'Not mine,' he corrected her. 'It belongs to the *contessa*.'

She was very still for a moment, her thoughts whirling blankly. The idea that he could be married had never even crossed her mind. Not, of course, that it made the slightest difference...

She said brusquely, 'Then she has my sympathy.'

'Why?' His brows lifted enquiringly. 'Is the car so difficult to drive?'

'Certainly not,' Lucy snapped. 'I meant that I—I pity anyone who's involved with a—a Lothario like you.'

'You imagine, perhaps, that Lothario was an Italian.' Giulio Falcone shook his head again. 'You are wrong, *signorina*. He was the invention of an English dramatist. Just as you seem to be inventing me,' he added, his tone dry.

'It doesn't take a great deal of imagination,' Lucy retorted. 'Nina was right, after all. You Italian studs are all the same.'

'The looks of a dove and the tongue of a wasp,' he said silkily. 'An intriguing combination.'

'Not for much longer.' Lucy swung the case off the bed. 'Will you loan me your—*contessa's* car to drive to Pisa, please?'

'No,' he said. 'I will not.'

She lifted her chin. 'Right—then I'll walk there.'

'In that dress?' He surveyed her mockingly. 'You'd be lucky to get half a kilometre. Even if the police did not stop you first,' he added, almost casually.

'I planned to change, given some privacy,' she said. 'I don't think jeans and a shirt would make me liable to arrest.'

'No,' he said. 'But there is the matter of trespass, which you seem to have overlooked.'

Fright was building up again, making her stomach churn. Her fingers tightened almost convulsively round the handle of her case.

She said jerkily, 'You can't be serious, *signore*. I—we acted in good faith. We didn't know this was your house.'

'That is hardly a defence,' he said. 'Especially when added to the acts of vandalism committed against my possessions.'

She couldn't argue. Her knowledge of Italian law was nil. Perhaps it ws one of those countries where you were guilty until you proved yourself innocent, she thought faintly.

She tried again. 'But you can't put all the blame on me. There were others involved.'

'True,' he said softly. 'But they have gone, and you, *columbina*, are the only one left to make the recompense I require.'

'You think I'm like them—like Nina and the others.' Her voice shook. 'But I'm not—I swear to you.'

'I believe you.' He lifted a negligent shoulder. 'Otherwise I would not want you.'

The amber eyes, hooded, watchful, swept over her, lingering on her breasts, the curve of her hips, the slender line of her thighs.

The dark face was coldly, almost dispassionately absorbed. Like his namesake, the falcon—the ultimate predator—with its prey in sight, and helpless, Lucy thought wildly, her body trembling, her brain teeming with desperation.

She said, 'You have no right—no right at all to keep me here against my will.'

'I think, under the circumstances, I have any rights that I choose to assume, Lucia *mia*.'

'Don't call me that.'

Giulio Falcone frowned. 'I was told it was your name.'

'Yes, but I didn't give you permission to use it.' She stood her ground, glaring at him.

'A minor detail,' he said softly. 'At such a time.' He paused. 'And when we are already on terms of such intimacy.'

'Because I ran to you for help?' Lucy asked scornfully. 'In that situation I'd have run to Frankenstein's monster.'

'No,' he said. 'Because you have been occupying my room. Sleeping, *mia bella*, in my bed, which presumably you chose out of all the others. Doesn't that establish some kind of bond between us?' He watched the shocked colour storm into her face and laughed. 'Don't tell me you hadn't guessed.'

'Think what you like.' Lucy gritted her teeth. 'But I'll never spend another night in it, or anywhere else under your roof.'

'I don't think that is your choice,' he said. 'Make me the restitution I require, and I promise that afterwards you will be driven to Pisa, your air fare paid, and a suite at the best hotel put at your disposal while you await your flight.'

'No deal.' Lucy made her tone brief and cutting. 'I am not for sale, *signore*.'

'And I am not buying, *signorina*. But I am prepared to—hire you for a while.'

'You disgust me.' In spite of herself, her voice trembled. 'Call the police, why don't you? Even jail would be better than another minute in your company. And I shall have my own story to tell them too,' she added bravely.

'In my bedroom—in that dress?' He sighed. 'I think appearances would be against you, Lucia.'

'Your wife might take a different view,' Lucy flashed. 'Or does she take your lousy, deceitful behaviour completely for granted?'

'It would be worth keeping you here if only to teach you to speak civilly,' Giulio Falcone said grimly. 'Anyway, you are under a misapprehension. I have no wife.' He paused. 'You are also ludicrously wrong about my motives for detaining you.'

He saw the sudden bewildered question in her eyes and smiled sardonically. 'The little comedy is over between us, *signorina*. My interest in you, alas, is more practical than romantic. I hope you are not too disappointed.'

She said between her teeth, 'Not in the slightest—if I had the least idea what you're talking about.'

'Actually, it's quite simple. I have a problem to which you could provide the solution.' He gave a slight grimace. 'Early yesterday, my sister was in a car accident. Neither she or the two children were badly hurt—cuts, bruises and shock, that's all. But the *governante*—the nanny—was not so fortunate. She broke her leg, and has to spend some time in the clinic.

'Fiammetta wishes to come here to rest and recuperate, but there is no one now to look after the children, and Marco and Emilia can be more than a handful.'

He spread his hands. 'I thought, of course, that Maddalena would be here to take charge until Alison recovers. The children are accustomed to her.' He paused. 'But, of course, there is no Maddalena. Only you, Lucia.'

'Me?' Lucy swallowed, aware that relief was being overtaken by a curious sense of deflation. 'But I'm not a nanny.'

'No,' he said. 'But you are here at this moment. You have admitted you owe me a debt you cannot pay. In turn I have ruined your holiday.' The amber eyes looked into hers, and she felt her heart thud suddenly and painfully. 'Tell me truly, Lucia, do you really wish to leave Tuscany so soon, when you could stay here, and be paid for doing so?'

'I couldn't possibly,' Lucy denied, trying to control her flurried breathing.

'Why not? With my sister and the children, you would be well chaperoned, if that is your concern.'

Lucy saw the amusement in his eyes, the sensuous curve of his mouth, and decided it would be safer not to explore that particular avenue.

'But I'd be totally unsuitable,' she protested instead. 'You don't know anything about me, after all.'

'You are unused to children, perhaps?'

'Well, no,' she said reluctantly. 'I have nephews.'

'Of what age?'

'Six and four,' she admitted, an involuntary smile curving her mouth. She saw him assimilate that betraying tenderness, and added hastily, 'But it's still out of the question.'

'I don't see why. Marco and Emilia are slightly older, it is true, but they have had a bad experience and they need someone who will care, as well as give them companionship.' He added softly, 'In spite of your temper, Lucia, you do not strike me as heartless.'

She said shakily, 'That's emotional blackmail.'

He shrugged. 'You say you cannot be hired, and will not be bought. What else is left to me?'

She tried again. 'But your sister may have other ideas.'

'Fiammetta, as usual, will take the line of least resistance. And this is an emergency. They will be released from the clinic tomorrow morning, and will be coming straight here. I cannot allow them to find a scene of such devastation.'

'And this is where I come in?' Lucy's tone was hollow.

'Until tomorrow, when I can mobilise help from the estate, certainly.' He gave her a measuring look. 'If this had been a genuine rental, you would have been expected to keep the house clean and tidy, after all.'

She bit her lip. 'I suppose so. But if all you want is a glorified housemaid-cum-nanny, why did you pretend—let me think...?' She halted, vexed with herself for asking.

'Because you were so ready to believe that I was just some—latter-day Casanova.' The firm lips twisted slightly. 'The temptation to confirm your worst fears became quite irresistible, believe me. But while you are in my employment and under my roof you are quite safe.' He flicked a glance towards the tumbled bed. 'Unless, of course, you insist.'

She was angrily aware that her face had warmed again. 'I don't,' she said tersely.

'Then I suggest you find yourself another room.' Both his tone and smile were pleasant, and untinged by even a modicum of regret, which, oddly enough, seemed to increase her annoyance.

She met his gaze stonily. 'So, if I agree to help out, you promise that will cancel all obligations between us?'

'More than that,' he said. 'I will ensure you suffer no financial loss as a result of Moressi's trickery.'

He paused. 'You will also take with you, I hope, some unforgettable memories of Tuscany, as well as the undying gratitude of the Falconese,' he added sardonically.

'Naturally, that would be one of my main considerations.' Her tone was sarcastic.

Giulio Falcone inclined his head gracefully. 'I knew you would see things my way.'

'Did you?' Lucy gave him an assessing look. 'Tell me, *signore*, are you related to the Medici by any chance?'

His mouth twitched. 'Only on my mother's side, *signorina*,' he returned silkily. 'Why do you ask?'

She shrugged. 'I gather they were hard men to refuse in their day. And so are you, Count Falcone.'

'Then don't refuse me.' He smiled at her, reminding her unnecessarily of the power of his attraction. 'And I don't use my title, unless I have to. Call me Giulio.'

Oh, no, she thought, the breath catching in her throat. That was an intimacy she didn't need.

Aloud, she said, 'I don't know what to say—what to do...'

'Then obey your instinct, *columbina*.'

Instinct was telling her to get out while she could. To put herself at the furthest, safest distance possible from this man. From his smile. From the charm that seemed to reach out to her like a caressing hand. From the sheer sexual charisma that turned the blood in her veins to warm honey. And which, she reminded herself, he seemed able to exercise at will.

Somehow, she heard herself say, 'Very well, I'll stay. But only till you can find someone else.'

'*Grazie*, Lucia.' His smile deepened, half-mocking, but wholly disturbing. 'And now I suggest you change out of that dress—before I forget all my good resolutions.'

For one long moment, his eyes stripped her lazily and quite deliberately. Then he raised his hand to his lips, blew her an amused kiss, and walked out of the room.

Lucy watched the door close behind him, and said loudly and clearly from the bottom of her heart, 'Bastard.'

Her first action, naturally, was to find another room. She chose one at the furthest end of the house from his, regardless of the fact that it was also the smallest.

Quite suitable for a servant's quarters anyway, she told herself, swinging her case onto the narrow bed.

Her pulses still seemed to be behaving oddly. She couldn't believe how easily she'd allowed herself to be wound up. How could she have thought, even for a moment, that someone like Count Giulio Falcone cherished even marginal designs on her?

The trouble was that at each of their prior encounters she'd been at some kind of disadvantage, which in turn had stopped her thinking rationally. That was the only explanation. And it provided a kind of marginal reassurance.

She still wasn't sure why she'd agreed to stay, however, except that there didn't seem to be much alternative. He was a wealthy and powerful man, who could probably be ruthless.

But it wouldn't be for long, she appeased herself. No doubt his sister would find a replacement nanny from some domestic agency when she'd recovered from the shock of the accident. And then the whole incident would dwindle into a little adventure to be laughed over ruefully back in England. Although not with Nina and the others.

And now to get out of this damned dress.

Lucy twisted round, feeling for the zip and tugging it downwards, but nothing happened.

'Oh, come on,' she muttered under her breath. 'You can't be stuck.'

But the zip, apparently, had other ideas, and remained exactly where it was. With a sigh of frustration, Lucy decided she'd have to cut herself out.

She was searching for her nail scissors, when there was a peremptory rap on the door, and Giulio Falcone walked in.

'So this is the sanctuary you have chosen.' He glanced around. 'A little cramped, don't you think?'

'I think it's ideal,' Lucy returned with a coolness she was far from feeling.

'As you wish.' He shrugged. 'But why are you still not ready? I was going to show you where the clean linen is kept.'

'Just give me general directions,' Lucy said tersely. 'I'll find it myself.'

'Is there a problem?'

'Nothing I can't handle.' She straightened, scissors in hand.

He surveyed them enigmatically. 'If you need to defend yourself, the range of knives in the kitchen might serve you better.'

'Nothing of the kind,' Lucy said crossly. 'My zip's stuck, that's all.'

'Then allow me.' He walked over to her, and turned her so that her back was to him.

She stiffened. 'I can manage.'

'Stand still.'

His breath was warm on her exposed skin as he bent closer to examine the erring metal strip.

'A thread has been caught,' he murmured. 'I think I can free it.'

Lucy waited rigidly, trying not to flinch as his cool fingers slid under the edge of the dress and touched her back.

'Don't be so nervous,' he chided softly, laughter in his voice. 'This must be better than attacking yourself with scissors.'

Not, Lucy thought with gritted teeth, necessarily.

He was infinitely too close to her, in the exact situation she had wanted to avoid. In the wall mirror, she could see his intent dark face, his lips only a fraction away from her bare skin. She found herself remembering, starkly, the feel, the taste of his mouth on hers, and was swept by a wave of longing she could neither control nor excuse. The movement of his hand against her spine as he tried to release the trapped fabric only increased her silent torment.

She said huskily. 'Could you hurry, please?'

'I am trying to be careful. I don't want to damage the material.'

'It doesn't matter.' She moistened her dry lips with the tip of her tongue. 'I'm never going to wear it again.'

'Truly?' He shrugged. '*In tal caso...*' He took the edges of the dress's neckline in his hands and pulled at them sharply. There was a harsh, splitting sound as seams and stitching gave way, then the entire bodice slid gracefully but inexorably from Lucy's shoulders, baring her to the waist.

For a stunned second she was motionless, then, with a small wail of horror and embarrassment, she snatched at the ruined fabric, dragging it up over her breasts.

Giulio Falcone stood back, watching her struggles, amusement dancing in his amber eyes, along with something deeper and more dangerous.

She said thickly, 'How could you? Oh, God, how dare you do such a thing?'

He shrugged. 'I merely followed your instructions. I am hardly to blame if the result did not meet your expectations.' He paused. 'Although it exceeded mine,' he added, half to himself.

'Get out of this room.' She was close to embarrassed tears. 'Get away from me. I should have known I couldn't trust you.'

'Then you'd be wrong.' His voice was stern. 'If I was the villain you imagine, you'd be in bed with me now, and we both know it, so let there be no more pretence about that.'

He paused again, his mouth twisting. 'As it is, I'm going to tell myself, *mia bella*, that you don't have skin like moonlight, or breasts like flowers waiting to be gathered by a man's hands, and go downstairs.' He added laconically, 'I'm going to make coffee. If you want some, join me.'

He sent her a brief, impersonal nod and walked out.

Lucy sank down onto the edge of the bed. In a reeling world, she was certain of only one thing. She could not risk remaining at the Villa Dante. She had to get away.

She lifted her head and looked at her reflection in the mirror. A stranger with dishevelled hair and eyes wide with confusion stared back. A stranger huddling the remnants of her dress against the pallor of her half-naked body.

'Skin like moonlight . . .' The remembered words sent an aching shiver through her body.

She thought, Let me get through tonight—just tonight. And realised it sounded like a prayer.

CHAPTER FOUR

WORK, and more work, Lucy told herself with grim determination. That's the answer. Keep busy—keep out of mischief.

Not that Giulio Falcone could be described as anything so innocent as mischief, she amended stormily as she changed into the comparative demureness of jade-green leggings and a matching sweatshirt, and kicked the discarded red dress into the corner of the room. He was danger—sheer and unequivocal. And she was all kinds of a fool to let him get to her like this.

Survival was the name of the game in this situation, and she knew enough about that, even if men like the Count were an enigma to her. A mystery, she told herself tersely, that she had neither the right nor the inclination to solve.

By keeping busy—concentrating on the task in hand—. she could stop herself thinking—wondering about him. And once the children arrived her time would be filled anyway, she reminded herself. Their presence would provide her with a measure of safety at least until she could make her escape.

She found all the clean bedding and towels she needed in a huge linen press at the head of the stairs. Sachets of dried herbs had been tucked amongst them, and she sniffed appreciatively as she collected her first load. However foolishly Maddalena might have behaved over her nephew, her housekeeping had been faultless, she thought wistfully.

The rooms the others had been using looked as if they'd been swept by a tornado, with unmade beds, cupboard doors swinging open, and empty drawers up-ended onto the floor, along with discarded hangers.

Wet towels decorated the bathrooms, with trails of dusting powder, and there were smears of hair gel and moisturiser on the mirrors and tiled surfaces.

Gritting her teeth, Lucy launched herself into the task of restoring order. Most of it was cosmetic, anyway, she realised as she made the bedding into loose bundles for future laundering. Luckily, they hadn't occupied the Villa Dante long enough to create the kind of mess that had to be scoured away.

Her own room—his room, she corrected herself tersely—she left until last. She stood outside for a long moment, oddly reluctant to proceed. Then, steeling herself, she pushed open the door.

The room was safely empty, and, apart from the unmade bed, tidier than the others. She felt obscurely glad of that.

The long window was open to the night, and some faint current of air made the drapes billow into the room.

She walked over to the window, intending to close it, and paused, staring up at the star-sprinkled velvet of the sky.

People said that one's fate was written in the stars, she remembered wryly. But she could see no pattern, no rhyme or reason for what had befallen her over the past twenty-four hours in those chilly, far-off specks of light.

The moon, on the other hand, looked close enough to touch, spilling silver light like a swathe of satin across the distant hillside.

'Skin like moonlight...' The words seemed to echo and re-echo in her mind. Her hand lifted slowly, and touched the curve of her breast.

For a moment, she was still, then she wrenched herself back to earth with a faint shiver, aware as never before of the silence of the encircling night. In daylight, the Villa Dante's quiet isolation had been something to prize.

But in darkness it only served as an unwanted reminder of her vulnerability...

Suppressing another shiver, she pulled the window shut and secured the latch. And, as she did so, she saw reflected in the glass a shadow moving in the room behind her.

The cry of alarm choked in her throat as she swung round, the precariously balanced armful of bedding sliding to the floor, spilling sheets and pillowcases at her feet.

'You're very nervous.' Giulio Falcone was totally at ease, even faintly amused as he walked forward from the doorway.

'Can you wonder?' Lucy said crossly, her heart thudding as she bent to retrieve the linen. 'I wish you wouldn't creep up behind me like that.'

His brows lifted. 'I came upstairs in the usual manner,' he pointed out with a certain hauteur. He paused. 'You seemed lost in thought.'

'Yes.' Lucy summoned a strained smile. 'Well—I have a great deal to think about.' She tried to sound brisk. 'And now I really must get on.' She moved purposefully to the side of the bed and began to strip off the sheets.

He said, 'You may leave that.'

'Beds don't change themselves.' Oh, God, she thought. I sound like the whimsical housekeeper in some ancient TV series.

'Then let it stay as it is.' The faint smile playing about his lips deepened as he saw her straighten slowly and send him a questioning look. 'Or do you think, *mia bella*, that I would object to sleeping with the scent of your skin, your hair on my pillow?' he asked softly. 'I promise I would not.'

She was angrily aware that she'd been lured into blushing again. She said, with an assumption of calmness, 'You gave me a job to do, *signore*. This is part of it.'

'Then it must wait,' he dictated. 'The coffee is ready, and I've prepared some food for us as well.'

Lucy's eyes widened. 'You can cook?'

He said with a trace of impatience, 'I am not the effete aristocrat you seem to think. I have learned, over the years, to be reasonably self-sufficient. I can even make my own bed,' he added drily. 'So come now and eat.'

'But we can't sit down to a meal in the middle of the night,' Lucy objected.

'Why not? If an appetite exists, it should be satisfied.' The amber eyes swept over her. 'Or don't you agree?'

Lucy bit her lip. She suspected the question had little to do with food, and that he was being deliberately provocative again, but to challenge him would undoubtedly lead her into deep waters, and probably make her look ridiculous.

So she followed him reluctantly downstairs. As they passed the open door to the dining room, she saw that it had been restored to its former shining splendour.

'Oh!' she exclaimed. 'I meant to do that next.'

'And now there is no need,' he returned. 'All the same, I hope you won't object if we eat in the kitchen.'

'I'd prefer it,' she said coolly. 'Isn't that where servants belong?' And she registered his swift frown with inner satisfaction.

But her jaw dropped when she saw the omelette he'd produced, succulent with fresh herbs, ham, tomatoes, peppers and cheese. Clearly he'd used everything in the fridge. And warmed some bread as well, she noticed weakly as she sat down. Not to mention opened a bottle of wine.

'I can't eat all this,' she protested as he put a plate in front of her. 'I'll be awake for the rest of the night...' Her voice trailed away in embarrassment as his brows lifted in overtly mocking speculation.

'You think so? Well, eat anyway. Build up your strength.' His smile touched her like silk. 'You will need it.'

The words seemed to hang in the air between them, half-threat, half-promise.

Lucy stiffened. 'May I ask why?'

'To handle Marco and Emilia, of course.' He picked up his fork. 'What else, *columbina*?'

His smile seemed to mock her, and if Lucy hadn't been suddenly so ravenous she'd have thrown the plateful of eggs in his face. Instead, she decided it would be infinitely safer to pursue the impersonal topic of her future charges.

'Are they so bad?' she asked, savouring her first mouth-watering forkful.

Giulio Falcone reflected for a moment. 'Not so much bad as over-indulged,' he decided laconically. 'Sergio, their father, is the disciplinarian in the family, but his work takes him away a great deal, which unfortunately leaves the children to the tender mercies of Fiammetta.' He sighed. 'She is, you must understand, as lazy as she is charming... and altogether too susceptible to outside influences,' he added with a slight frown.

Lucy's brows lifted. 'That's an odd thing to say about your own sister.'

'Ah.' The Count poured some wine into her glass before she could stop him. 'But then, she is not strictly my sister. She is the daughter of my father's second wife, now his widow.'

Lucy digested this along with another greedy mouthful of omelette. 'In other words, your stepsister.'

'*Sì.*' He nodded, lifting his glass. '*Salute.*'

She returned the toast uncertainly, taking only a cautious sip, conscious of the need to keep her wits about her, unfuddled by alcohol, or anything else.

'So the *contessa* you mentioned is actually your stepmother?'

'Yes.' The word was clipped, the firm mouth suddenly harder.

No love lost there, Lucy silently deduced. Aloud, she said, 'Will she be coming here too?'

'No. She lives in Rome for most of the year, and spends the summer mainly in Zurich and the South of France.' He added unemotionally, 'She is bored here and visits as little as possible, although I insist she attends the celebrations after the vintage. The workers on the estate expect it.'

'How could anyone hate it here?' Lucy said, half to herself. 'It's like heaven.'

Giulio Falcone shrugged a shoulder. 'The two faces of the Villa Dante.' His smile was thin-lipped. 'As the poet himself might have said—for you, Paradise, but for Claudia, Purgatory.'

'Yet the Fiat belongs to her. You said so.' Lucy frowned slightly. 'If the *contessa* comes here so rarely, why does she bother with a car?'

He shrugged again. 'As an escape route,' he said. 'Away from the tedium of the vineyards and country life to visit friends in Florence and Siena. Shopping, gossip and cards are her favourite pastimes.'

Lucy heard the edge of contempt in his voice.

She said slowly, 'We can't all like the same places— the same things...'

'This was my father's favourite retreat.' The dark face was brooding. 'Until, that is, Claudia's advent into his life, after which his visits were kept to a minimum,' he added tautly.

Lucy said haltingly, 'If your stepmother likes people— company—I can see why this wouldn't be much of a refuge.'

He looked at her sombrely. 'At your age, what do you know about needing a refuge?' he demanded.

'Perhaps more than you think,' she muttered, feeling the muscles in her throat tighten uncontrollably.

There was a brief silence, then Giulio Falcone reached across the table, tracing the pale circle on her finger where Philip's ring had been. His touch was light, but a faint tremor shivered through her nerve-endings just the same.

'What are you running from, little one? An unhappy marriage?' he asked quietly.

'No.' Lucy shook her head vigorously to disguise her instinctive reaction. 'We—we hadn't got that far—fortunately.'

'Fortunate indeed,' he murmured. The amber eyes glinted at her. 'So what went wrong?'

She shrugged. 'He met someone else.' She gave a small, painful smile. 'Someone with more to offer.'

'He told you that?'

'Not in so many words. He wasn't that cruel. But I— I drew my own conclusions.'

'And you are still sad?'

Am I? she wondered. Suddenly she wasn't sure. Philip seemed to belong to a different time—another existence. She barely recognised her own emotions any more.

Abruptly, she pulled her hand away. 'Of course. It was a—whole part of my life.'

'*Non importa,*' he said softly. 'A few weeks of Tuscan sun, *mia bella*, and that mark will soon vanish.'

Lucy tucked the offending hand away on her lap, under the edge of the table. Out of harm's way, she told herself sternly, aware of the swift hammering of her pulses.

It occurred to her that unless she was careful she could leave Tuscany not merely marked but scarred for life— the pain Philip had caused a mere pin-prick by comparison.

A few weeks, she thought, was far too long for safety. She had to get away, and soon.

She took a breath. 'To get back to the children,' she said carefully. 'Won't there be a language problem? My Italian is practically non-existent...'

'It doesn't matter.' His hand gestured dismissively. 'They are both bilingual. Much of their childhood has been spent in Britain and the States, and Sergio has insisted that they speak English as much as their mother tongue. On that score at least there will be no difficulty,' he added, half to himself.

'I see.' Marco and Emilia were clearly the children from hell, Lucy thought resignedly as she forked up the last succulent piece of omelette. She decided on another change of subject. 'Your own English is very good, *signore*,' she offered politely.

'It could improve,' he said, with a grimace. 'And it should, as so much of our bank's business is transacted in your country. Also, I have lived there for varying periods throughout my life. But not recently.' The amber eyes met hers quizzically. 'Otherwise we might have met before.'

To look away would be a sign of weakness, Lucy decided breathlessly. 'I don't think so.' She managed to keep her voice sedate. 'We move in very different worlds, after all.'

He inclined his head in acknowledgement. 'But sometimes worlds collide, Lucia. Don't you believe in the force of destiny?'

'I think I prefer to stick to practicalities.'

'So tell me about the practical side of your world. You have a job?'

'Yes. I trained in graphic design and now I work in advertising.'

'Your company?'

She told him, and his brows lifted in amused respect. 'Impressive, Lucia. But you don't think it possible that my bank or one of our associates might come to your organisation to publicise the services we offer.'

She smiled. 'I think it unlikely, *signore*. And almost certainly unnecessary.'

Giulio Falcone laughed. 'You could be right. So let me be practical again. My English has grown a little—rusty—is that the word? Perhaps you could give me some lessons.'

Lucy lifted her chin and met his teasing glance head-on. She said composedly, 'I doubt whether I could teach you a thing, *signore*. Besides, I shall clearly have my hands full with Marco and Emilia.' She pushed her chair back and rose to her feet, summoning a bright, meaningless smile. 'And now I'd better get some rest. Big day tomorrow.'

Giulio Falcone courteously stood up. 'Sleep well, Lucia. But remember this.' His voice followed her as she went to the door, almost stumbling in her attempt not to hurry. 'Destiny has placed you in my world now. And there is nowhere for you to run to.'

Not, Lucy thought as she went up to her room, a thought to induce restful slumber.

She shut the door behind her with some force and leaned back against its panels, sudden tears pricking at her eyes.

She said aloud, her voice ragged, 'Damn him.'

In spite of her forebodings, Lucy went to sleep almost as soon as her head touched the pillow.

When she awoke next day, sunlight was pouring like thick warm syrup through a gap in the shutters and pooling onto the shining floor. For a moment, she was totally disorientated, then as memory returned she sat up with a jerk.

Hell, she thought frantically. I must have overslept.

She grabbed her watch from the night table, and saw with horror that it was past ten o'clock.

Hardly the right time for a working day to start, she told herself, swinging her feet to the tiled floor. She could only hope that her autocratic employer might have overslept too.

She showered swiftly, debating what in her limited wardrobe would be considered suitable for a surrogate nanny. In the end, she settled for a brief button-through denim skirt, topped by a white blouse, scoop-necked and sleeveless. She brushed her hair back severely from her face, securing it at the nape of her neck with a tortoise-shell clip, and pushed her feet into flat leather sandals.

She looked neat, she decided without enthusiasm, and relatively businesslike.

As she passed Giulio Falcone's room, she saw that the door was open and the bed, though rumpled, was un-occupied. So he'd beaten her to it after all, she thought, with a faint grimace.

She was expecting some sarcastic remark or even a silken reprimand when she arrived downstairs, but, to her surprise, there was no sign of him. The place seemed deserted, although the coffee-machine had been in use, she saw when she entered the kitchen.

She poured herself some fruit juice from the pitcher in the fridge and sipped it slowly, leaning against the frame of the back door, looking out into the courtyard which housed the garages. Giulio Falcone's car was no-where to be seen, she realised, although the Fiat waited in its usual place.

Above Lucy's head, a flowering vine hung mo-tionless, not a leaf or a petal stirred by so much as a passing breath of air. She put up a hand and lifted the hair away from the back of her neck with a small sigh. This, evidently, was going to be a scorchingly hot day.

The kind of day she'd come to Tuscany to enjoy, if only things had been different. If only, she thought with longing, she were a free agent again.

Free. The word shivered through her consciousness, and took hold.

She looked again at the Fiat and drew a breath. Well, why not? she argued inwardly. Her jailer had disap-peared and left the prison gates open, so why stay a moment longer than she had to? Why should she carry the can for everything when Nina and co. had escaped? She'd made all the amends that were strictly necessary by getting the bedrooms ready for the new arrivals.

Last night, she'd been almost mesmerised into accepting his terms, she thought defensively. But now it was daylight, and she was wide awake and ready to fight back. To escape. Because there was somewhere to run to after all.

And the noble Count Falcone could simply find someone else to look after his charming stepsister and her spoiled brats, she told herself decisively.

She said aloud, 'I'm going home—now. While I still can.'

She left her unfinished juice in the kitchen and sped back upstairs to her room, where she piled her belongings haphazardly into her case.

Then, for a long moment, she stood at the top of the stairs, heart hammering oddly, ears stretched for the least indication of his return. But there was only silence, so, resisting an impulse to tiptoe, she went downstairs and out to the car.

To her surprise, it was locked. I don't remember doing that, she thought, rummaging in her bag for the keys. In view of the villa's isolation, security hadn't seemed a major issue.

But the keys didn't seem to be there. Irritated, Lucy tipped her bag out on the bonnet of the car and sorted through the contents, only to remember with a sinking heart that Nina had driven back yesterday from Montiverno.

Oh, no, she groaned inwardly. Don't say she's taken them off with her. She thought back, trying to remember their return to the villa. She'd gone straight to her room—*his* room—and Nina had been with her. She was almost certain she could recall the other girl tossing

the keys down onto the dressing table—the clatter as they
skidded across its polished surface.

If that was where they'd been, there was an outside
chance that they'd be there still. That Giulio Falcone
hadn't noticed their presence. He'd have been too tired
last night, she thought. And this morning, with luck,
he'd have had other things on his mind.

At any rate, it was worth a look. She hid her case
behind a big stone trough brimming over with flowers
and flew back into the house, taking the stairs two at a
time.

One glance at the dressing table told her that her optimism was ill-founded. Apart from the mirror on its
polished stand, the surface was totally clear.

Lucy could have screamed with frustration.

Calm down, she adjured herself. Maybe they're still
here—in a drawer, perhaps.

Feverishly, she wrenched open the top drawer and
scanned the contents: hairbrushes, a leather case con-
taining cuff-links, and a selection of fine linen hand-
kerchieves. In the next drawer down were silk socks.
Which, she decided grimly, was as far as she went.

She pushed an errant lock of hair back from her
forehead as she considered the situation. It was faintly
possible that the keys, thrown carelessly, might have
skidded all the way across the top and fallen into the
gap between the dressing table and the wall.

She tried to ease out the heavy piece of furniture so
that she could look behind it, but it defied her efforts.
Panting, Lucy dropped to her knees, awkwardly craning
her neck as she tried to peer underneath it instead.

From the doorway behind her, a familiar vioce
drawled, 'Checking for dust, *mia bella*? What a paragon
you are.'

Lucy jumped violently, and straightened, muffling a
shriek as she banged her unwary head on a drawer's
protruding handle.

Oh, God, she thought sickly. Why on earth hadn't she heard him returning? She could only be thankful that he hadn't actually caught her going through the rest of his things.

She said between gritted teeth, resisting the urge to rub the aching spot on her head, 'That's the third time you've scared me out of my wits.'

'It's the third time I've found you in my room,' Giulio Falcone retorted silkily. 'I shall begin to think, Lucia, that you can't keep away.'

Lucy got to her feet, glaring at him. 'Then you'd be wrong,' she said crisply. A glance at her bare left wrist gave her inspiration. 'Actually, I was looking for my watch. I thought perhaps I'd left it in here.'

'I regret, no.' He came further into the room. Pale grey trousers hugged his lean hips and accentuated the length of his legs, and his coral polo shirt had been left unbuttoned at the neck. Lucy, assimilating all this, was aware of a slight flurry in her breathing.

He looked her over unsmilingly. He said. 'You were wearing your watch last night, I think.'

'Oh, was I?' She gave a little shrug. 'I couldn't be sure.'

His scrutiny of her intensified. He said, 'Did you hurt yourself just now?'

'Not at all,' she said stoutly. It was a lie. In fact, she felt as if she was going to have a lump like the dome of St. Paul's. She produced a feeble imitation of a bright smile. 'Well—I'll go and continue to search elsewhere.'

She had to pass him to reach the door. His hand closed round her arm, halting her effortlessly.

He said quietly, 'I did not intend to startle you, and for that I apologise. Among other things, I went to the vineyard to ask Franco's wife, Teresa, to cook for us on a temporary basis.' He paused, then added with a faint smile, 'I thought I would be back before you awoke.'

Lucy lifted her chin. She said coolly, 'I'm sorry to have put you to so much trouble, *signore*. It won't happen again. If you'd care to specify a time for my duties to begin, I'll make sure I'm awake and available in future.'

The smile deepened. 'Why the outrage? I am not the first man to see you in bed, after all.'

'That's not the point,' she said stonily. 'I happen to value my privacy.'

He shrugged. 'Then I must respect it.' The amber eyes met hers in unnerving confrontation. 'I promise, *columbina*, never to enter your bedroom again—without an invitation. Is that the assurance you want?'

Lucy forced herself to look away to the open door. 'It will do, I suppose.' She glanced down at his detaining hand. 'Now, may I go, please?'

'On the other hand,' he went on softly, 'you have my full permission to enter my bedroom whenever you wish, and stay—just as long as you desire.'

He strolled over to the dressing table. 'I hope you find your watch,' he added casually. 'It's so annoying to search and search, to no avail.'

Numbly, Lucy watched him produce first his own car keys then those of the Fiat from his trouser pocket. Slanting a smile at her, he tossed both bunches into the air and caught them, before dropping them unhurriedly into the top drawer. He was watching her stunned reaction, she realised, in the mirror.

He said mockingly, 'Before you continue your hunt, may I suggest an ice pack for the bump on your head, Lucia?' He paused. 'Who knows? It may also have a cooling effect on your temper.'

And his laughter followed her, even through the door she slammed behind her and down the long passage to the fragile security of her room.

CHAPTER FIVE

THE room was already like an oven, and there was no-where to sit but on the bed, which did nothing to improve Lucy's mood.

Giulio Falcone was a snake, she raged inwardly. A devious, conniving bastard, who'd outthought and out-manoeuvred her all along the line. In fact he'd made a total fool of her, and she hated him.

Which, admittedly, was a far safer attitude than her previous naïve response to his attraction. Hard work alone wasn't a sufficient defence against the smile that curled the corners of his mouth, or the amber fire that glowed in those extraordinary eyes. She'd found that out to her cost last night.

No, she thought, she needed hate as an extra—maybe even a final line of defence, until some day, somehow, she could teach him a lesson he would never forget.

She emptied her bag onto the bed and went through its contents slowly and methodically, calculating how much she had in lira, how much in travellers' cheques. Her driving licence was in her wallet. Maybe she could—just—afford to hire a car to take her to the airport. But where could she stay if no flight was immediately available? And how long could she manage?

The questions seemed to chase each other in her brain. What a fool she'd been not to bring her credit card, she thought ruefully, yet at the time it had seemed a sensible move, a disincentive to over-spending, particularly since she was contemplating a change of flat when she returned home.

She looked through the other pockets in the wallet, just in case she'd slipped the card in after all in a moment of aberration, but all she found were receipts, a library ticket and, tucked away and forgotten in an inside pocket, a photograph of Philip.

She took it out and looked at it. A month ago, it would have destroyed her. Now she sat and studied it almost objectively. It was one she'd taken on the flotilla holiday, the first day she'd felt well enough to venture up on deck. Philip, of course, was already bronzed, his blond hair bleached by the sun, totally accepted as one of the gang. He was leaning against the rail, smiling for the camera, his blue eyes crinkling in the way she'd always loved. But he was looking past her, not at her, focused on a different horizon. She could see that now, so clearly.

I was always swept along behind him, in his wake, she thought. Never at his side, as I should have been. As I wanted to be.

She took a breath, ripped the photograph cleanly in half, and dropped it into the waste basket.

The tap on her door brought her defensively to her feet. No need to ask who was there, of course.

She said stonily, '*Si?*'

'My sister is here, Lucia. Will you come down with me to meet her?' As she hesitated, he added, 'However angry you are with me, please remember that the children have been badly frightened, and need you.'

Fuming, Lucy swept to the door and threw it open. She said icily, 'That is a shameless piece of manipulation, and you know it.'

He flung up a hand. '*Mi dispiace,*' he said, without a trace of penitence. 'But I have been accused of worse things. Now stop sulking, please, and come downstairs.'

He turned away, and Lucy took an impassioned step forward, only to bark her shins on her own suitcase, which had apparently deserted its refuge behind the flower trough and was now standing dejectedly outside her door.

No prizes for guessing how, she thought malevolently, glaring after his retreating figure. She pushed the case into her room and closed the door on it.

When she got to the stairs, the hall below seemed full of people and noise. There was a uniformed driver stolidly bringing in more luggage than Lucy had ever seen in her life. There was a tall blonde girl, dressed with the kind of careless elegance normally encountered only in the pages of the glossiest magazines, talking very fast and gesturing rapidly. There was a small boy with dark curly hair capering about and shouting, and a slightly older girl in tears.

She almost cannoned into the Count, who had paused halfway down the stairs and was standing as if he'd been turned to stone, staring across all this chaos to the open doorway. In which, Lucy saw with foreboding, there was yet another newcomer.

She was a much older woman, matchstick-slender and exquisitely dressed, her silver hair formally and immaculately coiffed. She was looking round her with mingled authority and disdain.

'Claudia,' Giulio Falcone said softly, and at the sound of his voice a magical silence seemed to fall on the rest of the company. *'Che sorpresa.'*

The woman in the doorway smiled. 'My dear Giulio,' she purred. 'Naturally I am here for my daughter.'

Although she spoke in Italian, Lucy had no difficulty making an accurate translation. The *contessa*, she thought, had a curious voice; it was husky, with a metallic undertone—like honey eaten off a steel spoon.

The *contessa's* eyes, vibrantly dark under heavy lids, looked past him up the stairs to Lucy herself, who had a searing impression of having been tried and found wanting. She said austerely, 'And who is this girl?'

Giulio replied in English, his tone cool and deliberately casual, 'This is Lucy Winters, my dear Claudia, who has agreed to replace Alison, and look after the children and keep house for us, until we can make other arrangements.'

The arched brows swept up. '*Dove* Maddalena?'

Giulio shrugged abruptly. 'There was trouble with Tommaso. She left—rather suddenly.'

Claudia Falcone made an exasperated sound. 'Was there no suitable local woman, rather than another English girl?'

It occurred to Lucy that she made the word *inglesa* sound like an expression of contempt.

Giulio shrugged again. 'Teresa has agreed to come and cook for us,' he said. 'But she has her own family to consider. She cannot take on other duties as well.'

'But if she was paid—' the *contessa* began, to be interrupted by the younger woman.

'Mamma, of course we want another English girl, so that the children's lessons won't be interrupted. We should be grateful to Giulio for the trouble he has taken to find a suitable replacement for our poor Alison.' She gave Lucy a cordial smile. 'How do you do, *signorina*? It is good to meet you. I am Fiammetta Rinaldi.'

'But who is this young woman, and where has she come from?' the *contessa* demanded impatiently. 'What are her credentials? Is she fit for this kind of responsibility?'

Fiammetta's tone held a touch of exasperation. 'Mamma, don't fuss so much. I am sure Giulio would engage no one whose references were not impeccable.'

Oh, no? Lucy questioned in silent irony, and found Fiammetta addressing her again.

'This has not been a good way to make your acquaintance, *signorina*—or may I call you Lucia?—but the past forty-eight hours have been—trying.' She pulled a faintly comic face.

She was indeed enchantingly pretty, Lucy acknowledged, with enormous pansy brown eyes and a frankly sexy mouth. Even the strip of sticking plaster on her forehead could not detract from her overall sparkle.

'More than merely trying,' came the *contessa's* voice, with the metallic note even more strongly in evidence. 'The accident could have been terrible—a tragedy. The life of my only grandson was placed at risk.'

Lucy saw the older child flinch, her tear-stained face hurt and fleetingly hostile, and in that moment she knew she would never like Claudia Falcone.

She said politely, 'Then your granddaughter was not in the car at the time, Contessa Falcone. That was lucky.'

Her words fell into a suddenly tense silence, broken by the little boy dancing up and down. 'Emilia was in the car,' he announced importantly. 'But she cried. She wasn't brave like me. And today she was sick.'

He gave a realistic impression of his sister's mishap and hooted with laughter. Emilia began to cry again, noisily, and her grandmother turned away, her face frozen with distaste.

Lucy, biting her tongue with an effort, decided resignedly that it was high time to intervene properly. She walked down the stairs to the Count's side, and touched his arm.

She said quietly, 'Perhaps you'd take the ladies into the *salotto*, *signore*, while I see to the children. Emilia at least will need to be washed and changed.' She looked at Fiammetta. 'Perhaps you, *signora*, know which case her clothes are in?'

Fiammetta gave the mountain of luggage a frankly hunted look. 'Unfortunately, no.' She spread her hands apologetically. 'Alison did the packing, you understand.'

And someone quite apart from the lovely Fiammetta, Lucy deduced wryly, was going to have to do the unpacking.

She said steadily, 'Well, until it's found, I'll just have to do the best I can.' She extended an encouraging hand to Emilia, whose sobs had turned to hiccups. 'Shall we go and make you more comfortable?'

The child's face was sullen and mutinous. 'No,' she burst out. 'I want Alison.' At Lucy's approach, she swung towards her grandmother, as if to bury her face in her dress, and the *contessa* stepped swiftly backwards, her hands moving in a gesture of repugnance and negation.

Giulio moved into the breach. He said gently, but firmly, 'Alison is not here, little one, so go with Lucia.'

'I won't. I won't.' Emilia seemed on the verge of hysterics. 'You can't make me!'

'You don't think so?' He swung the child up into his arms, hugging her, making a game of it, regardless of the condition she was in, then started up the stairs with her, Lucy following.

To Lucy's surprise, he carried Emilia straight into his own room, setting the little girl down in the adjoining bathroom, ruffling her hair as he did so. 'There you are, *cara*. Everything will be better soon.'

He looked at Lucy, brows raised. 'You can manage?' It was a statement rather than a question, and she nodded.

'Thank you.' She took a breath. 'That was—kind of you.' And totally unexpected, she added silently.

He shrugged. 'It had to be done.'

Lucy began to run the water into the tub. She said with a forced smile, 'You'll probably need to change as well.'

'Almost certainly,' he confirmed laconically. 'But it doesn't matter. With children these things happen.' Casually, he pulled his shirt over his head and tossed it into the adjoining linen basket, before giving Emilia a parting grin.

'Behave for Lucia, little one,' he commanded softly, and walked back into the bedroom, where he paused to select a fresh shirt from the *guardaroba*.

Lucy became suddenly, burningly aware that her gaze was following him, avidly drinking in every ripple of muscle beneath the bronzed skin. She smothered a gasp and turned away, concentrating her attention on the temperature of the bath-water, thankful that Giulio Falcone hadn't noticed.

Gawping like a sex-starved adolescent! she chastised herself mentally. For God's sake, pull yourself together, you idiot.

In spite of her uncle's admonition, Emilia was not disposed to co-operate. She was not, Lucy thought as she helped her out of her soiled clothing, a particularly prepossessing child, her current problems notwithstanding. She was thin and rather sallow, with a sullen expression and a small, pursed mouth. Unfairly, Marco seemed to have gained the lion's share in looks and grace, and Lucy suspected the little girl had been made well aware of that.

She complained that the bath-water was too hot, then too cold, and that the shampoo stung her eyes. She pushed the handspray away while her hair was being rinsed, drenching Lucy to the skin.

All in all, it was a memorable introduction to her new duties, Lucy decided grimly, struggling to lift Emilia's deliberately dead weight out of the bath. She wrapped the child in a bath-sheet, gave her hair a brisk towelling, and sat her on the bed, regardless of her protests, while she went to her own room to fetch her hairdryer.

To her surprise, she found her case standing out in the passage again. More astonishing yet, through the open door she could see a sour-looking elderly woman, dressed in black, hanging other sombre garments in the *guardaroba*.

Lucy checked. She said politely, 'Excuse me, I think there's been some mistake.'

She received a look of complete indifference in return. She tried again. 'This is my room.'

A shrug, and a muttered, *'Non capisco,'* was the only response.

'Now that I don't believe,' Lucy said roundly.

'Is there a problem?' The *contessa's* voice came from behind her, and Lucy swung round with a slight start. Creeping up behind people must be a family trait, she thought tartly.

She said, 'I seem to have lost my room.'

'Your room?' The older woman's brows lifted. 'But this room is always occupied by my maid when I am in residence. I need to have her near me.' Her smile was wintry. 'I'm sure you understand.'

'Of course,' Lucy said pleasantly. 'I'll move into one of the others.'

The *contessa* examined a fingernail with a certain amount of care. She said, 'Unfortunately, I have guests arriving this afternoon. All the rooms in the villa are needed. But there is the *casetta* in the grounds which Maddalena used. You will be quite comfortable there.'

Lucy stared at her. She said evenly, 'I'm supposed to be here for the children. I assumed Signora Rinaldi would want me near them.'

'But of course,' the *contessa* said smoothly. 'The children will share the *casetta* with you. It is an ideal arrangement. My daughter needs a few days' complete peace and rest to recover from the shock of the accident. Although she is an excellent and most affectionate mother children of this age can be so wearing, don't you find?'

'Presumably,' Lucy said, aware that she was trembling with anger, 'your visitors will cause no disruption at all to the household.'

The *contessa's* brows lifted in hauteur. 'My niece has been visiting Florence with a friend. Naturally I wish to see her.' She paused. 'As a temporary employee, *signorina*, you could hardly expect to remain under this roof and mix on an equal footing with our guests.' Her smile was bland. 'Although, to save our good Teresa inconvenience, you will be permitted, with the children, to join us for meals.'

She gave Lucy a long look. 'One of these days, *signorina*, you and I must discuss the circumstances in which you became so readily available for this job.'

Lucy picked up her case. She said, 'I suggest you ask your stepson, *contessa*. After all, anything I had to say would only be servant's gossip.'

Head high, feeling she'd scored a minor victory, she marched back along the passage to rejoin Emilia. She extracted the hairdryer and the adaptor from her case, and began to dry Emilia's hair, a process the child endured in smouldering silence.

'Now then,' Lucy said when she finished. 'Doesn't that look pretty?'

Emilia gave her reflection a look of total indifference.

'I am not pretty. I heard Nonna say that no one would ever believe I was Mamma's daughter, and that I look like a *fanciulla abbandonata*—a child from the streets.'

Lucy sighed soundlessly. She said gently, 'I'm sure she didn't mean it.'

'Nonna means everything she says. She wants Mamma to send me away to school to nuns who will beat me when I am naughty.' There was a note of real despair in the small, sulky voice.

Lucy said robustly, 'Then you'll have to be extra good, so there's no excuse for you to go.' She reached into her case and brought out a cream-coloured T-shirt with stylised flowers in red and gold cascading across the front. 'Until your own things turn up, would you like to wear this?'

Emilia looked down her nose at it. 'Does it belong to you?'

'Yes, but I've never worn it, so you won't be contaminated,' Lucy said lightly, trying to make a joke of it. 'And it would make a very pretty nightshirt,' she added. 'You can't sleep in a damp towel.'

Emilia looked mutinous again. 'I don't want to sleep,' she denied, the heaviness in her eyes belying her defiant words.

'Remember what I just said about being extra good?' Lucy popped the T-shirt over the child's head, and after only a superficial show of reluctance Emilia consented to allow herself to be tucked under the thin coverlet.

'How long are we going to stay here?' she asked, watching Lucy replace her hairdryer in its carrying case.

'That's for your mother to decide,' Lucy returned.

The child looked woebegone. 'We were going to the sea when that car hit us. I like it there. Here, there is nothing.' She sighed. 'But Mamma will do what Nonna says. She always does when my father is not here. I hope he comes back soon.'

I'll drink to that, Lucy agreed silently.

'This is Zio Giulio's room,' Emilia went on. 'Why am I here?'

Lucy smiled at her. 'Because our rooms aren't quite ready yet. We're going to stay in our own little house in the grounds.'

Emilia sat up in bed. 'The house that was Maddalena's?' Her voice was incredulous.

Far from being a waif, at that moment she bore a strong resemblance to the *contessa*, Lucy thought ruefully, but she gave a cheerful nod.

'That very one.' She lowered her voice conspiratorially. 'And we'll have it all to ourselves.'

Emilia stared at her, clearly weighing the ignominy of being relegated to the housekeeper's accommodation against the positive advantage of being away from her grandmother.

'But why can we not stay here?' she demanded at last.

'Because there are going to be other visitors,' Lucy explained. 'One of your cousins.'

'I have only one—Angela.' Emilia's mouth twisted petulantly. 'Of course, Nonna would ask her.'

Lucy bit back a smile at the world-weary tone. 'Don't you like her?' she asked, tugging down the lid of her case.

Emilia shrugged. 'It doesn't matter whether I do or not. It's Zio Giulio who has to like her.'

The words seemed to fall into an odd stillness.

'Why?' Lucy asked at last, aware that she was concentrating with unwonted fierceness on the clasps of her suitcase.

Emilia gave a superior little giggle. 'Because she's the girl Zio Giulio is going to marry, of course.'

Lucy felt suddenly as if she was trapped inside some vast, echoing vacuum. As if all sound, colour and sensation had vanished from the world, leaving her empty and desolate.

Across some wide and stinging distance, she heard herself say, 'Are they engaged?'

The child shook her head. 'No, but I heard Mamma say to Papà that Zio Giulio was only waiting for her—' her forehead creased '—to grow up and settle down.'

Lucy looked down at her hands. There were red marks where the clasps had dug into the soft flesh.

She thought with anguish, Oh, you fool. You stupid, pathetic idiot.

Aloud, she said calmly and quietly, 'Well, it's time you settled down as well. I'm going to go and make our new home ready for us.'

With a grudging nod, Emilia slid down in the bed. Lucy went into the bathroom to tidy up, closing the door behind her. She looked at herself in the mirror, noting almost clinically her pallor, and the wide, startled, unhappy eyes.

She said softly and fiercely, 'Well, what did you think? You knew from the start that he was only amusing himself at your expense. And now you've had it confirmed.'

She could only pray that Giulio Falcone had no idea how far she'd travelled down the road of no return to a hell of her own making.

No doubt he thought she was easy game—a woman recently rejected by another man. But if he thought she was in the market to be used—humiliated yet again—if he thought she was a pushover, then she would prove him wrong.

He might have been able to gauge her physical reaction to him, but oh, dear God, let him not have guessed the depth of her mental and emotional surrender.

She thought despairingly, Don't let me have fallen in love with him. Not that—never that.

It was in her own hands now. He must never know— she must never reveal by word or sign that he had the power to hurt her. Otherwise her time at the Villa Dante would be purgatory indeed.

And I thought I could hate him, she mocked herself bitterly. I thought I could make that my defence.

But how could things have moved so far and so fast— and with a man she hardly knew? It was ridiculous— incredible. She wasn't impulsive. She was steady and reliable, testing the ground before she moved. Her relationship with Philip had been based on secure foundations—or so she'd thought.

But what did I know? she lashed herself. A few days of that Tuscan sun Giulio had spoken of had already transmuted her, changed her into some unknown and challenging quantity.

Forty-eight hours ago, she thought slowly, she'd been unaware that Giulio Falcone even existed. Now she was enmeshed and helpless in a bitter web of jealousy and passion.

She tidied the bathroom like an automaton, pushing the used towels into the linen basket, wiping out the bath with a handful of tisssue.

If she left, if she actually, physically ran away, Giulio Falcone could not follow her. His fiancée's presence would see to that.

But wherever she went, however much distance she put between them, he would be with her in spirit, the demon on her shoulder, the restless yearning that could not be appeased.

I have to stay, she told herself. I have to see him each day with this Angela, the woman he intends to marry. I have to face the certainty of it. I have to burn out this need for him before it destroys me. To treat it as the pathetic infatuation it undoubtedly is.

When she eventually returned to the bedroom, she saw without surprise that Emilia had already fallen asleep.

She stood looking down at the little girl, aware of a tug of sympathy as she saw that a single teardrop had made its way down the small, sallow face.

You poor little soul, she thought with sudden anger. I'm not the only unhappy one. Damn him. Damn all these Falconese with their beauty and their careless cruelty.

But I won't let them get away with it. I'm going to stay here—and fight, even if the real battle's going to be against myself.

And, holding her head high, Lucy went downstairs.

CHAPTER SIX

To LUCY's relief none of the family was immediately in evidence, although she could hear the murmur of voices from behind the closed doors of the *salotto*, including Marco's childish treble.

In the kitchen, she found Teresa, a big, smiling woman, already clashing pots and pans with vigour. Lucy introduced herself matter-of-factly, fended off Teresa's flood of questions with apologetic incomprehension, and removed herself with tactful speed to her new abode.

It was hardly a spacious refuge, with two bedrooms and a tiny bathroom up a flight of wooden stairs, and a combined living room and kitchen at ground level, but it would do.

It would have to, she thought with gritted teeth as she tried to decide how to allocate the sleeping accommodation. The children were still young enough to share a room, so she determined to put both the old-fashioned single beds in the larger room, and herself use the folding bed with the rather solid mattress in the small bedroom. Even the *contessa* couldn't object to that, she thought grimly.

The doorways were narrow, but, with a lot of pushing and pulling, she eventually achieved her objective.

If ever I lose my job, I can always find work as a chambermaid, she thought, pushing her hair back wearily, and wincing faintly as her fingers encountered the bump on her head. Something else to hate him for.

She'd found the linen store, and was matching sheets and pillowcases, when she heard someone enter the *casetta* with a swift, forceful stride, and then Giulio

74

Falcone calling her name. For a moment, she experienced a cowardly urge to jump into the cupboard and hide.

Lunatic, she chastised herself caustically. You'll have to face him sooner or later.

She took three deep and calming breaths, then walked collectedly downstairs. He was standing staring around him, hands on hips, his face grim.

Lucy halted on the bottom step. I need the advantage of the extra height, she told herself. In fact, I need all the help I can get.

'Is something wrong, *signore*?' Her voice was cool.

'Everything, I would say, *signorina*,' he returned in savage mimicry of her own formality. 'I have come to apologise to you.'

Surprise jolted her. It was not what she'd expected.

'There's really no need—' she began, but he interrupted her.

'You are wrong, Lucia. There is every need.' His tone grated. Without doubt, he was very angry. 'I asked you to stay here to help Fiammetta and the children. I did not anticipate Claudia's descent on us, or that she would have invited—guests without consulting me first.' His mouth was compressed into lines of stone. 'Nor did I expect this.' He gestured contemptuously around him. 'I can only say, to excuse her, that she is a law unto herself, and has always been so.'

He took a deep breath. 'But her arrival, and its consequences, changes everything, naturally. Under the circumstances, I release you from our bargain. You are free to leave whenever you wish. I suggest the sooner the better.'

There was a silence.

It was almost funny, Lucy thought with detachment. Here she'd been, agonising over whether to go or stay, torn by indecision and the pain of love. And here was

Giulio giving her her marching orders without a second thought. Only she didn't feel like laughing.

She said quietly, 'And what happens to the children?'

'They have a mother and a grandmother. Between them—'

'Very little will happen. You admitted as much yourself,' Lucy said bitingly. 'To be frank, neither of them wishes to be bothered.' She lifted her chin. 'So— are you prepared to take the job on?'

He looked taken aback. 'I?'

'That's what I thought.' Lucy gave a decisive nod. 'In that case, I'm staying, *signore*, but only for the children's sake, and until you can find other help.'

He said quietly. 'That is impossible.'

'Why?' She paused, forcing herself to challenge his gaze.

'Because your presence would cause difficulties.' His tone was harsh. 'You are not aware of the identities of these—new visitors.'

'You're wrong, *signore*. I know exactly who is expected.' She actually managed a trace of cool amusement. 'And you really don't have to worry about a thing. I have no intention of being an embarrassment, if that's what you're afraid of.'

He stared at her, his whole attention sharply arrested. He said, 'You know? You have heard? But how?'

'Does it matter?' She was shaking inside, but she kept her voice even. 'It makes no difference to me, I assure you.'

'Then it should.' His eyes narrowed. 'Lucia, you don't have to pretend. Not with me.'

'There's no pretence about it.' Her nonchalant shrug took every ounce of strength she possessed. 'It was just— an interlude. I know that. Not to be taken seriously, and certainly best forgotten. That's what I plan to do. So please don't worry.'

'It seemed otherwise to me,' he said quietly. 'Forgive me, but I had the impression that it was more—far more than just an interlude.'

Lucy bit her lip. Humiliation was twisting inside her like a knife, but she kept her voice level. 'Then you're wrong, *signore*. But at least I hope we can agree that it's over. And that it's best to act as if—as if it never happened at all.'

'Brave words,' he said. 'But how will you feel when you are confronted by reality?' He spread his hands almost helplessly. 'I don't want to see you hurt, Lucia.'

I'm hurt now, she wanted to scream at him. Can't you see I'm bleeding to death?

She straightened her shoulders. 'Please don't trouble yourself any more. You—you're really taking something quite trivial far too seriously. And I'm sorry if I've given you a false impression of my feelings—my involvement. It really wasn't intentional.'

There was a taut silence. Then he said, 'I see.' His tone was courteous but impersonal. 'Clearly my original opinion of you was the correct one.' He allowed her to digest that for a moment, then pointed to two suitcases behind him. 'I have found the children's clothes,' he added.

'*Grazie,*' she said.

'*Prego,*' he returned carelessly. His smile was brief, not reaching his eyes. 'I wish you good fortune in your newest role, *cara*. I hope you don't find it too demanding.'

'Don't worry,' she said. 'I'll remember my place.'

He was turning to leave, but swung back to face her. 'Your place?' he echoed, his voice harsh with anger. 'I'll show you your place, *mia cara*.'

The endearment sounded like an insult. Two strides brought him to her. His hands clamped on her waist, pulling her forward so that she was pinioned against him, breast to breast. Then, for one endless moment, his mouth possessed hers, roughly, almost ravenously. Shocked, Lucy felt her lips yield, part helplessly under the force of his invasion.

But even as she acknowledged her surrender it was over.

Giulio stood back, releasing her abruptly, almost contemptuously.

He said, 'And now you have something else to remember. Another item of trivia for your collection.'

He strode out of the *casetta*, and the door banged shut behind him.

Lucy's pent-up breath escaped her in a quivering sigh. Slowly, she uncurled her fingers from the palms of her hands and flexed them carefully to reduce the ache of tension. Her head was throbbing badly now, and she felt close to tears of mingled rage and disappointment.

Even before that—violation of her mouth, his whole attitude had been an insult, she thought raggedly. Clearly he was scared that she would try to make capital out of what had passed between them with his future wife.

Did he really think she was that small-minded and spiteful? Yet what else could she really expect? Giulio, in fact, was taking the more realistic stance. They were, in spite of all that had passed between them, still virtual strangers to each other.

And the fact that she seemed to have every line of his lean, arrogant body etched on some inner consciousness, that the sound of his voice made her pulses do crazy things, that the touch of his lips and hands, even in anger, made her flesh clench in yearning—this—all this was her problem, and hers alone.

Except that, to her shame, he had guessed all the emotional turmoil she had wanted to conceal, she thought bitterly. Giulio had seen through her flimsy pretence as easily as if she were transparent.

And now he was clearly concerned that this Angela might do the same. Which was why he'd tried to hustle her off in that humiliating way.

But she'll never guess from me, she vowed silently. From here on in, Count Giulio Falcone was forbidden territory, and she would make sure their separate worlds never collided again.

Lunch, for Lucy, was a fairly tense occasion. Emilia, though reunited with her own clothes, was in a surly mood, and Marco, who'd had the undivided attention of his adoring grandmother for most of the morning, seemed bent on proving just how badly he could behave if he tried.

A beautiful child, but spoiled rotten, Lucy thought detachedly as she tried to prevent him transferring the contents of his plate to the dining-room floor.

The *contessa* kept up a constant stream of talk in her own language, her thin lips stretched in smiles, her hands gesturing restlessly. Fiammetta, clearly embarrassed, made several half-hearted attempts to switch the conversation into English, and draw Lucy into it, but these were swiftly overridden by her mother, who was at pains to ignore Lucy's presence altogether. It was an object-lesson in how to be rude, performed with the utmost charm.

And Giulio said nothing at all. He lounged in his chair at the head of the table, looking withdrawn and pre-occupied, toying with the excellent escalope of veal in spinach sauce that Teresa had prepared.

Lucy, risking one swift glance at him from under her lashes, supposed that he was thinking about Angela. Counting the minutes to her arrival, no doubt. She sighed soundlessly, and helped herself to more green salad.

When the meal was over, Fiammetta said instantly that the children must rest, prompting an immediate outcry from Emilia.

'I have used up all my sleep,' she protested. 'Marco can rest. I shall swim in the pool.'

'Not immediately after a meal, I'm afraid.' Lucy made the veto, and in return received a venomous look and a sharp kick on the shins under the table. Her smothered gasp of pain was masked by Marco's vociferous denial of his own weariness.

'Marco, *caro*.' Fiammetta put a languid hand to her head. 'Such noise.' She turned to Lucy. 'Lucia, could you do something—?'

'Of course she can,' the *contessa* broke in impatiently. 'That is what she is employed for. Take the children away, *signorina*, and amuse them.'

'There is no need.' Giulio pushed back his chair and rose. 'I am going down to the vineyard to talk to Franco. They can come with me. But only if they behave,' he added sharply as both children descended on him with whoops of joy.

'You are going out?' There was displeasure in the *contessa's* tone. 'But Angela will be arriving at any moment.'

'Then I can rely on you to make her—and her companion—welcome,' he returned coolly. 'They are, after all, your guests, my dear Claudia.' He left the room, a child hanging onto each hand, leaving behind him what Lucy supposed was a pregnant silence.

It was broken by the *contessa* with a small torrent of enraged speech, which Fiammetta interrupted with a gurgle of laughter. 'Mamma, have you not yet learned that Giulio is his own man, and that you cannot drive him? He will marry Angela when he is ready, and not before. In the meantime—' she gave a voluptuous and very wordly shrug '—they will both amuse themselves as they wish.'

Lucy felt as if she'd swallowed a stone.

'Her upbringing should have been left to me.' Two bright spots of colour burned in the *contessa's* face.

'Then there would have been no such amusements, and the matter would have been settled long ago.'

'Perhaps.' Fiammetta shrugged again, this time with indifference, then turned to Lucy who, for a number of reasons, was trying to edge unobtrusively from the room. 'Lucia, I have found some books and toys which Alison packed for the children among my luggage. If you come to my room, I will give them to you.'

Lucy had no choice but to agree. As they went up the stairs, Fiammetta slipped an arm through hers. 'Lucia, I want you to know that I am so grateful that you are here. Also that you must not pay too much heed if Mamma is—distant. The truth is she has no great love for the English. Her younger sister, Bianca, whom she greatly loved, married an Englishman, and died in your country after giving birth to Angela. Mamma blamed Bianca's husband, the hospital—everyone, but in fact it was no one's fault. It was a tragic accident which could have happened anywhere at any time. Only Mamma has never accepted that.'

Lucy said awkwardly, 'How terrible. I'm very sorry.'

Fiammetta rolled her eyes expressvely. 'It gets worse. She wrote to my uncle, offering—no, demanding—to take the *bambina* and bring her up herself, here in Italy. When he refused—*per Dio*—what an uproar. He has never been forgiven, believe me.'

Lucy stared at her. 'You mean, having lost his wife, he was also expected to give up his baby?'

'Mamma has a mind that runs on one track,' Fiammetta admitted ruefully. 'When she married Conte Falcone, both Giulio and I were only children. She hoped very much to bear another child—another son—and when it did not happen she decided instead that Giulio and I should marry.'

She shook her head. 'What an idea. Neither of us was the least in love with the other—although Giulio is very attractive,' she added, her full lips curving in a smile that combined mischief with sensuality. 'Besides, I never knew what he was thinking, and that drove me mad. But with Sergio I always know, so it is perfect.'

Lucy was startled by the frankness of these confidences. '*Signora...*' she began with reservation.

'Oh, so formal, and I cannot bear that. Alison is one of the family, and you must be too. Call me Fiammetta. You are wondering why I tell you these things?' She led Lucy into her bedroom and closed the door. 'It is not just gossip, you understand. There is something you must know, if you are to look after my children.' She paused. 'There is a big problem with Emilia.'

Tell me about it, Lucy thought ironically. She said quietly, 'I'm sorry to hear that,' and waited.

Fiammetta picked up a picture book, fiddled with it almost irritably and put it down again. 'When she was born, Mamma was pleased, naturally. Her first grandchild. But when Marco came—the longed-for boy—that was altogether different. She was crazy with joy—almost as if he were her own son. We thought, Sergio and I, that it would pass, but it has not. And Emilia sees it—and is jealous.'

She took a deep breath. 'One day, Mamma went into Marco's room and found Emilia standing by his crib with a glass in her hand. There was water everywhere—on the blanket—on his face. She said she was trying to give him a drink...' Her voice tailed away.

'Perhaps it was true,' Lucy suggested.

'Mamma did not think so. She was like a madwoman.' Fiammetta cast her eyes to heaven. 'She said that the glass could have been broken—accused Emilia of trying to harm Marco, and Emilia shouted back that we all loved Marco better than her and she hated him.'

Lucy said gently, 'A certain amount of sibling rivalry is part of childhood. My own nephews fight like crazy...'

'There were other things. When he could just walk, we found her taking him to our swimming pool—to teach him to swim, she said. Which she could barely do herself. If he had slipped...' She shuddered and put a hand to her mouth.

Lucy put a hand on her arm. 'But he didn't—and it must have been a long time ago.'

'That is what Sergio says, but I cannot forget it. Mamma will not allow it.' The pansy dark eyes were suddenly filled with tears. 'Each time Marco has a fall, or hurts himself, she makes me see that it could have been because of Emilia. That she might have hit him or pushed him. And that is not all. Recently Emilia has been stealing—oh, not a great deal—a few thousand lire from my bag, or from Mamma. But it makes me so anxious.'

She spread her hands. 'Mamma thinks we should send her away—to a school that deals with disturbed children. The Mother Superior is an old schoolfriend of hers, and a trained psychologist. Instead we've reached a—compromise. I hired Alison, on the understanding that she should watch particularly for Emilia and that if there were further—incidents we would consider the treatment this school could offer.'

Lucy swallowed. 'Have you mentioned this to Giulio—I mean Count Falcone?'

'No.' Fiammetta shook her head. 'Giulio was only a young boy—fourteen years of age—when Mamma married his father. He had loved his mother very greatly, and he found it difficult to accept that any other woman could take her place. And Mamma—made mistakes, also. It would be hard now for Mamma to share this trouble with him—to admit that her granddaughter could be—sick in some way. If he was married—if he had children—the family relationship might be closer. He might understand more...'

'Well, perhaps things will be different—' Lucy's voice sounded peculiarly toneless '—when he marries—Angela.'

'Poor Mamma.' Fiammetta's sudden smile was like the sun breaking through clouds. 'She did not succeed in matching Giulio to her daughter, so now it has to be her niece. One way or the other, he must not escape.' She giggled. 'It has become almost an obsession with her.'

'And do the happy couple have no say in the matter?'

Fiammetta shrugged. 'It will be no hardship. Angela is very beautiful, and Giulio—well, you must have seen for yourself. He is a man that any woman would want, even without his money and his power.'

She lowered her voice conspiratorially. 'I thought it would happen three years ago, when he was in London and they met constantly, but he would not commit himself, other than to say she was too young. Since then, they have both seen other people, but in the end they will take each other.'

She nodded. 'And she will make him a good wife, I think, because she can share his world, his business interests in a way I never could.' The smile spread into a grin. 'Sergio does not bother me with such things.'

Lucy was not surprised. Fiammetta had warmth and charm, but was probably not overburdened with brains, or any great depth of character. And she was certainly under the thumb of the *contessa*. She had lost count of how many times Mamma had been mentioned.

'But this time Angela has made Mamma angry,' Fiammetta went on, unconsciously reinforcing Lucy's opinion, 'by bringing her latest man-friend here. Never before has she flaunted one of her other relationships in Giulio's face like this.'

'Maybe she's trying to force the issue by making Count Falcone jealous,' Lucy suggested woodenly.

'Perhaps you are right.' Fiammetta clapped her hands. '*Bravo*, Lucia. How clever of you.' She gave an enchanting gurgle of laughter. 'And how will he retaliate, I wonder? I think the next few days are going to be very interesting—no?'

I think, Lucy decided detachedly as she returned to the *casetta* with her arms full of books and games, that they're going to be almost more than I can bear.

Over the next hour, she busied herself with putting the children's clothes and other items away, and trying to dispel the forlorn and spartan air of the living area with colourful pots of flowers, brought in from the courtyard, and a bright cloth for the table.

She was sure that it still wouldn't look anything like home to Emilia and Marco, but at least she'd tried, she told herself, with a brief sigh.

She had closed the shutters against the hot afternoon sun, but the air inside the *casetta* was stifling just the same, she thought, easing the neck of her blouse away from her damp skin. As she had some time to herself, she might as well cool off beside the pool.

She changed into a black bikini, covered it with a loose silk overshirt, and stuffed her dark glasses, sun lotion and book into a bag.

The whole villa seemed to be sleeping in the sun as she made her way through the gardens. No bees droned in the dense banks of lavender which surrounded the pool, and even the crickets were silent. Not a leaf stirred as she went softly past, the sound of her own breathing alone disturbing the intense, burning quietness of the afternoon.

For a moment, she stood at the top of the steps, looking down at the tranquil turquoise water, remembering the events of the previous night—the music, the raucous laughter, her own terror—with a shiver of revulsion, allowing this new and unaccustomed peace to enfold her like the billowing silk of her wrap.

As well as the cushioned loungers and umbrellas, there was a pile of thickly padded mattresses for sunbathing. Lucy spread one of them under the sheltering branches of the ancient tree which provided a modicum of shade at one end of the pool, then discarded her shirt and slid into the water, feeling it caress her grateful skin like cool satin. She swam one slow, easy length, then lifted herself out onto the tiled surround and sat wringing the water out of her hair.

Fiammetta's artless confidences were still revolviong in her mind, however much she might try to dismiss them, or tell herself forcefully that they were none of her concern.

Because, for good or ill, she was concerned, she acknowledged with a small aching sigh, and had been ever since that first unfortunate encounter with Giulio in Montiverno.

The mere thought of him was enough to send a tingle vibrating through her senses, however many kinds of fool that might make her.

With a snort of self-derision, she got to her feet and walked around the pool to the waiting mattress, running her hands through her damp hair as she went.

She picked up her towel and began to blot the moisture from her arms and legs, then paused, her mental antennae suddenly, oddly alert.

From somewhere above her, behind the blue wall of lavender and the thickly ranked roses, had come a faint rustle, like a passing breeze. Only the air was still. And, as Lucy listened, she heard the rattle of a dislodged pebble, as if rolling away from a careless foot.

She stiffened, scanning the barrier of flowers for telltale signs of movement. She called, 'Is anyone there?' But there was no answer. A total hush had descended once again.

I must have been imagining things, Lucy thought, spreading her towel on the mattress and stretching out on it, face down. She pillowed her head on her folded arms and closed her eyes, letting the silence enclose her.

She found a succession of images turning in her mind—Emilia's wan face, Fiammetta's anxious eyes, the *contessa's* expression of haughty disdain. And, above all else, Giulio Falcone, his amber eyes sparking fire, his mouth rigid in anger or curving in a smile. The instinctive, inherent grace of his lean body. The masked strength of the practised, beguiling hands.

Lucy closed her eyes more tightly and saw tiny coloured lights dance behind her lids. But she could not dispel his image.

His shadow, she thought drowsily, always there in the sunlight. On the edge of every thought and every dream.

And she knew that she was lost, irrevocably, and for all time.

CHAPTER SEVEN

LUCY seemed to be floating on some warm current of air, her whole body totally relaxed, as she looked down at the rolling golden landscape beneath her. Her arms were wings, and she was a bird in flight, a dove, swooping earthward, then spiralling up to freedom.

But somehow she knew that her freedom was an illusion, and destined to be short-lived. Hovering above her was the shadow of a falcon, the predator whom she could never escape, twist and turn as she might.

Then she heard her name called softly through the sunlit air. Was aware of hands smoothing her feathers, stroking her into submission. Touching her with complete mastery.

Suddenly this was no dream, but sheer reality, drawing her up through the layers of sleep to swift, shocked consciousness—and to Giulio, who was kneeling over her, massaging sun lotion into her shoulders and down the length of her back, his fingers practised and very firm.

'What the hell do you think you're doing?' Lucy sat up, frantically grabbing at her bikini-top, which he had apparently unhooked.

'Preventing you from being roasted alive, I hope.' His tone was caustic. 'The sun moved while you were asleep, little fool.'

'Wouldn't waking me and telling me so have been the more obvious course?' she demanded furiously, the fact that he was correct in no way mitigating her sense of outrage.

'Perhaps,' he agreed, the amber eyes slumberously

amused under their heavy lids. 'But not nearly as enjoyable, believe me.'

She bit her lip, mortified. 'And I suppose it was you playing peeping Tom earlier,' she accused. 'Not a becoming role for the master of the house.'

'What are you saying?' The dark brows drew together.

'Oh, don't pretend,' she said scornfully. 'Just how long were you lurking in the bushes, spying on me?'

'Have a care, Lucia.' His voice was silk on steel. 'There are limits, even for you. I arrived a few moments ago, intending to swim. If you had not been lying in the full glare of the sun, I would have respected your privacy and left.'

Lucy, struggling to re-hook her top, surveyed him. He was still wearing the same clothes he'd put on that morning.

'Swimming, *signore*? You don't seem to have a costume—or a towel.'

'At this time of day, Lucia,' he said softly, 'I usually have the pool entirely to myself, so I can forget about such tiresome niceties.' Watching her, his mouth curving faintly, he began to unbutton his shirt. 'You wish me to demonstrate?'

She had a potent mental image of what Giulio Falcone would look like stripped, and her mouth went dry.

'No,' she said forcefully. 'Absolutely not.' She snatched up her shirt and got to her feet. 'I—I'll leave you to it.'

He rose too, laughing, and lifting his hands in mock surrender. 'Don't run away, *columbina*. Enjoy the sun—now you are protected against it—and also your freedom, while you can.'

'Oh, heavens.' Lucy looked belatedly and wildly around her. 'The children—where are they? Are they all right?'

He gave her a curious glance. 'They are quite safe—playing with Franco's brood. Teresa will bring them back to the house when she comes to prepare dinner presently. There's no problem.'

'Are you sure Signora Rinaldi will agree?'

He frowned. 'She has never objected before,' he said. 'What is this?'

Lucy bit her lip again. 'I don't want to be accused of neglecting my duties, that's all,' she returned stiffly.

'Now, I wonder if that is the whole truth?' he said softly. 'No matter; I shall find out eventually.' He paused. 'But stay, please, anyway. I don't want to feel I have driven you away.'

Lucy stood, irresolute, acutely conscious of the expanse of honey-gold skin revealed by the scanty bikini, knowing that he was aware of it too. Knowing that he'd been touching her, running his hands over her naked back.

Giulio waited for a moment, then sighed. 'Lucia *mia*, please stop clutching that shirt as if it was a shield. It is not necessary.'

'No?' She lifted her chin. 'You have a short memory, *signore*.'

'On the contrary.' He paused again. 'If you wish me to apologise for my conduct this morning at the *casetta*, then I will. Under the circumstances, I had no right to touch—to kiss you. I admit it. But I refuse to do penance for the sun lotion,' he added. 'That was a necessity.'

She said rigidly, 'You had no right, whatever the circumstances.'

He shrugged. 'Then perhaps I was simply making good use of what precious little time is left to me,' he retorted. 'I can hardly be blamed for that.'

'Except that I'm not here to be used. I'm fulfilling my side of our bargain, and nothing else.'

'Now your memory is at fault, *mia cara*,' Giulio drawled. 'The bargain between us is cancelled, as I made clear. From now on, you remain at your own risk.'

She said quietly, 'So be it. But you'll understand if I prefer not to take unnecessary ones by staying alone with you in an isolated place.'

His face hardened. 'First of all you accuse me of leering at you from the bushes like some callow adolescent,' he said, 'and now I am a potential rapist, it seems.'

'I didn't say that...'

'But the implication was there,' he cut back at her. 'The implication that you cannot trust me. That I cannot be alone with you without taking something you do not wish to give.' He shook his head. 'You are wrong. I have never taken anything from any woman that has not been freely offered, and you, Lucia, will be no exception to that rule.'

She said thickly, 'Then why don't I feel safe?'

'Perhaps because you do not trust yourself.' His tone was almost grim.

She gasped, and colour flared in her face. 'How dare you?'

'Because, unlike you, I am not afraid of risks.' His shrug was negligent. 'Now, go on with your sunbathing, while I take my swim. The length of the pool should be enough space between us. Unless, of course, you wish to join me in the water?'

'Thank you,' she said, 'but I thought you realised last night that I'm not interested in that kind of—adventure.'

'And I thought you realised I was teasing you.' He pulled his shirt over his head, unzipped his grey trousers and stepped out of them to reveal brief black swimming trunks. 'Does that appease your sense of decency, *columbina*?'

It did her no favours at all, Lucy thought, the breath catching in her throat. He was magnificent—well muscled, without an ounce of surplus weight.

'It doesn't tempt me to stay.' She forced herself to speak calmly, even casually, while her heart was thumping to beat the band. She slipped on her shirt, and began to button it with clumsy fingers.

'And what is that supposed to achieve?' he demanded cynically. 'Do you think I have no memory—no imagination?'

Lucy's eyes sparked with sudden fire. 'I know you have no conscience, *signore*, otherwise you wouldn't behave like this. You couldn't.' She picked up her bag. 'Another reason why I choose not to stay here.'

'And I have no choice in this?'

'Yours is already made.' She looked him straight in the eye. 'I'm here to work, *signore*, not to provide you with—passing amusement.'

'That,' he said harshly, 'was not my intention.'

'I'm not interested in your intentions. Let's talk about responsibilities—obligations—instead. You seem to have forgotten those.

'You are wrong, Lucia.' The amber eyes travelled over her slowly, dismissing her flimsy covering, surveying her with frankly sensual reminiscence. 'I don't forget a thing. How could I?'

She swung her bag over her shoulder. Her voice sounded ragged. 'You're not being fair, *signore*.'

As she walked past him, he reached for her. His fingers closed round her wrist. Held her.

He said softly, 'What can ever be fair in this situation? Lucia, look at me, my little, sweet fool.'

The air surrounding them seemed suddenly to be quivering, shimmering with an intensity which had nothing to do with the sun's glare.

The blood in her veins was slow and heavy, the pounding of her heart a pain in her chest. She had only to turn towards him, she thought dazedly. Only to turn...

She heard, as if from nowhere, a girl's laugh, deep and throaty, rippling out, snapping the tension between them. Shattering the dream.

'Playing your usual games, Giulio, darling?' She was standing on the steps, looking down at them. She was dark, and very beautiful, her frankly voluptuous body showcased by a shift dress in stinging pink, cut low over her full breasts, and finishing well above the knee. 'And who is your latest playmate?'

Lucy's head went back, and the breath left her body in a silent gasp, as if she'd been struck and winded.

No need to guess who the newcomer was. It was—it had to be—Angela. Giulio's cousin by marriage and intended wife.

Only she was no stranger. Lucy had seen her before, and quite recently too. In London, coming out of a restaurant in Knightsbridge. With Philip.

Who was here too. Standing on the step behind her, his face frozen in disbelief and something bordering on horror.

And I know, Lucy thought, a bubble of hysteria welling up inside her, exactly how he feels.

She disengaged her hand sedately. She said, 'I'm the hired help, *signorina*. We had a slight disagreement over terms of employment, that's all.' She flashed a bright, meaningless smile around her. 'And now, if you'll excuse me...'

And she went past them, up the steps, two at a time, without looking back.

'Oh, God,' Lucy whispered to herself as she paced the living room at the *casetta*. 'This can't be happening. It can't be true.'

The shock of seeing Philip so unexpectedly had almost bowled her over. She'd always assumed that when they ran into each other again she would be devastated. But that hadn't been her reaction at all. Dismay had been her uppermost emotion, and embarrassment too. Because, without a doubt, this was one big complicated mess.

All she could concentrate on now was damage limitation. Clearly Angela had no idea that she and Philip had ever been involved. So far, so good.

Nor was there any reason for Giulio to equate her own lost love with Angela's English boyfriend, she thought. She surely hadn't given that much away in those late-night confidences.

There seemed every chance that they could both remain in blissful ignorance. Least said, soonest mended, she decided, as she would tell Philip immediately she got the chance.

As for herself, she would maintain the lowest possible profile as the children's nanny, and let things take their course. Although there was little doubt in her mind what that course would be.

There was bitterness in her throat and a pain in her heart as she thought of Angela, so beautiful, so confident, radiating sexuality. Her smile had been amused as she'd surveyed the telling little scene in front of her, her glance at Lucy totally dismissive.

As Fiammetta has suggested, she and Giulio took each other's little diversions in their stride, it seemed.

But where did this leave Philip? she wondered uncomfortably. Was he just a passing amusement too, or was his affair with Angela the real thing, at least as far as he was concerned?

And what did Angela herself feel? She'd taken Philip, but did she really want him? Set against Giulio, he had little to offer. An aptitude for adventure sports and a propensity for hard work didn't count for much against old money, power and a family tree that went back to the Renaissance. Or was Angela, as Lucy had prophesied, simply using him to spur Giulio into making a proposal?

She sighed. The way things were going, she could end up a two-time loser, she thought wretchedly.

Except, of course, that Giulio had never been hers to lose. And that was what she had to remember at all costs, if she was to keep her sanity.

It was a relief when Teresa, full of smiles, arrived with the children and the performance of getting them washed and presentabe for dinner could get under way. It stopped her from thinking. From pondering the imponderable, and coming up with no answers at all. Or none that she could bear, she amended with a pang.

'When I am a man, I shall have a vineyard,' Marco announced ebulliently.

'In the meantime concentrate on drying between your toes,' Lucy counselled. She gave Emilia a quick smile. 'And what are you going to do with your life?'

Emilia shrugged. 'I shall find a rich husband, like Zia Angela.'

'Better get a new face first.' Marco gave a crow of laughter, followed in short order by a yelp of real pain. 'She pinched me.' Accusingly he held out a chubby arm for Lucy to inspect the tell-tale fingermarks.

'If you didn't say unkind things to your sister, maybe it wouldn't happen,' she pointed out as she hung the damp towels on the rail.

'You are supposed to take my side, not hers.' The small face was outraged.

'I don't intend to take sides at all,' Lucy said cheerfully.

'Then I shall tell Mamma what she did, and she will get into trouble.'

Lucy stole a swift glance at Emilia. Her face was set and sullen, but there was apprehension in her eyes, and Lucy felt reluctant compassion for her.

She wrinkled her nose thoughtfully. 'People who tell tales are horrid.'

'But Nonna says that Emilia must be punished if she is bad to me.'

'And what happens when you are bad to her?' Lucy asked calmly.

'Nothing,' Emilia burst out. 'Because I am always blamed.'

'I have an idea,' Lucy said. 'Why don't you both try to be pleasant to each other for just one day?'

The idea was greeted without enthusiasm.

'And if we do?' said Marco. 'What will you give us?'

'I'll wait till you've done it,' Lucy said grimly, 'and then decide. Now, go downstairs and play quietly while I change.'

She had just emerged from the tiny shower cubicle when she heard a crash and a shriek from downstairs. She wrapped a towel round herself sarong-style, and dashed down. One of the plants she'd brought in earlier lay on the floor, its terracotta pot smashed, and soil and broken blooms everywhere.

'Who did this?' she demanded.

'It was Emilia. She threw it at me.'

'I did not.' Emilia was red with anger. 'He was playing with it, and I told him to stop, so he dropped it.'

'Liar,' Marco yelled.

'What is this name-calling?' an icy voice asked from the doorway, and Giulio walked in.

'One of them broke this plant,' said Lucy, crushingly conscious of her lack of attire. 'They each blame the other. Not a good start to the new regime,' she added, looking fiercely from one sulky face to the other.

'Lucia said if we are nice to each other for one whole day she will give us a reward,' Marco told his uncle.

Giulio's mouth twitched. 'Bribery, *columbina*?'

'You have to start somewhere.' Flushing, she yanked hastily at her slipping towel.

Giulio looked directly at the children. 'Well, little rascals, if you can do this great thing, I will reward you myself.' He pretended to think. 'How about a picnic?'

'*Sì, sì,*' they chorused, jumping round him like puppies, all the sulks magically forgotten.

'But it is for Lucia to say if you deserve it, agreed?' He smiled coolly at Lucy. 'Fiammetta says the children may go and talk to her while she dresses. I have come to collect them—and just at the right moment, it seems.'

'Yes.' The towel was perfectly adequate, but Lucy felt absurdly flustered under his lingering scrutiny. 'Thank you,' she added.

'*Prego.*' As the children scampered ahead into the evening sunlight, Giulio turned back suddenly from the door. The smile that curved his mouth now was intimate, and a little wry. He said softly, 'And if I am good for a day, *mia cara*, will you reward me?'

The blood burned in her face. She said quietly, 'I think I'm on safe ground, *signore*. Twenty-four hours is a long time.'

And, with as much dignity as she could muster in a bath-towel, she turned and retreated upstairs, aware that he was watching her every step of the way.

From the window she watched him cross the courtyard, her fist pressed to her mouth so tightly that her lips felt bruised.

Twenty-four hours, she thought. A very long time. Long enough to fall in love. Long enough to discover the kind of pain that could tear you apart, and leave you suffering for all eternity. Long enough to realise you wanted to die.

Only it was never that simple. You just had to go on living—and hurting.

'Hating him,' she whispered rawly, 'would have been so much easier.'

Lucy expected to find the family already assembled in the *salotto* when she eventually made her reluctant entrance, but to her surprise Philip was the only occupant.

He was standing staring moodily out of the window, holding a Campari and soda, but he turned as she came in, glaring at her.

'What's the game, Luce? What are you doing here?'

'I have a temporary job as nanny to Signora Rinaldi's children.'

'That's rubbish, and you know it. I think you came here deliberately, to embarrass me.' He shook his head, more in sorrow than in anger. 'I'm disappointed in you, Luce. I thought you had more dignity—more pride.'

'Don't flatter yourself,' Lucy advised him curtly. 'I had no idea that your girlfriend had any connection with this household. In fact, the entire family were strangers to me up until yesterday.'

'You expect me to believe that? That you've taken a holiday job skivvying for a crowd you don't even know?' He laughed rudely. 'Pull the other one.'

'I really don't care what you believe.' How strange, she thought, that it should be true. 'But it happened.' She paused. 'I got ripped off and needed some cash. They needed a nanny.' She gave him a minatory look. 'But as far as I'm concerned, Philip, you and I are strangers too. Our meeting like this is an appalling co-incidence, but it doesn't have to be a disaster.'

'I suppose not,' he said crossly. 'Though it's on a par with the rest of this ghastly trip.' He sat down heavily on one of the sofas. 'It was meant to be a romantic holiday for two,' he complained. 'And then, as soon as we got to Florence, Angela suddenly turned into this culture vulture. It was a nightmare. We actually had to queue to get into the Uffizi, and, as for that guy's statue of David, there must be dozens of the damned things. Every time I turned round there was one looming over me.'

Lucy wanted badly to laugh. She said gently, 'I think most of them are copies and the original is in the Accademia.'

'Oh, well, you would know, of course.' He subjected her to a critical look. 'I haven't seen that before.' He sounded almost pettish.

Lucy glanced down at the floating wraparound skirt in blue, green and turquoise, which she'd teamed with a simple scoop-necked white top. 'No, it's new. I bought it for this trip.'

'Hardly nanny gear,' he said sourly. 'But I suppose you know what you're doing.' He drank some of his Campari. 'To be honest, Luce, I wasn't expecting to stay with Angie's relatives, either. She never said a word about it in London.' He brightened slightly. 'But I suppose it's a good sign—wanting me to meet the family.' He lowered his voice. 'But the aunt—the *contessa*—she's a bit of a blight.'

'I find her charming,' Lucy said mendaciously.

'There's no accounting for taste.' He favoured her with another, longer look. 'I've got to hand it to you, Luce. You're looking terrific.'

'Thank you,' she said drily.

'I mean it.' His eyes narrowed. 'As fanciable as you were when I met you.'

She said calmly, 'Or until you started fancying Angela instead.'

'Oh, come on, Luce.' He gave her the boyish grin which would once have turned her legs to jelly. 'We had some good times together, you must admit.'

'Did we?' She glanced at her watch. Where the hell was everyone?

'You know we did.' He put down his drink and stood up. Lucy watched these manoeuvres with disfavour.

She said, 'Whatever you're planning, Philip, forget it. And stop calling me Luce. I've always hated it.'

He stopped in front of her, staring down at her as if he'd never seen her before. And maybe, she thought, he never had, at that.

'Well, well,' he said unpleasantly. 'Aren't we suddenly high and mighty? Could it be because you think the great Giulio Falcone is making a move on you? I wasn't blind to what was going on down at the pool when we arrived. According to Angela, he's famous for his casual flings, but his standards are usually higher.'

The smile she summoned cost Lucy a great deal. 'Thanks. I—I'll consider myself warned.'

She heard a sound behind her and turned. Giulio was standing in the doorway watching them, his face expressionless.

He said, 'Good evening. It is a poor host who keeps a guest waiting.'

'Oh, that's all right.' Philip moved back towards the sofa, distancing himself from Lucy. 'Angela said I should help myself to a drink.'

'But of course. Usually there would be someone to wait on you, but at the moment we are having servant problems.' He walked to the side-table where an array of bottles waited. 'May I offer you something, Lucia?'

'Just some fruit juice, please.'

He said mockingly, 'But how virtuous.'

He poured orange juice from a pitcher and added ice, before handing it to her. It was only the tinkling of the cubes against the side of the glass that made her realise her hand was shaking.

Philip downed the remainder of his Campari. 'I think I'll go and see what's keeping Angela.'

'The eternal problem of what to wear, no doubt,' Giulio said courteously, pouring himself a whisky as Philip went towards the door.

He left a silence behind him that could have been cut with a knife.

Lucy made herself drink some of the fruit juice, forcing it down her taut throat, waiting for whatever was to come.

When at last he spoke, his voice was almost gentle. 'Keep away from him, Lucia. He is not for you.'

Do you think I don't know that? she wanted to scream at him. How can you be so blind? Don't you know I'd have died rather than have him touch me?

Instead, 'Is that a warning?' she asked, keeping her tone deliberately light.

'No.' He shook his head. 'An order—which you will obey.'

'Because he belongs to your cousin Angela?' she challenged.

His smile was suddenly harsh, almost feral. 'Perhaps. Until she tires of him. She is cursed with a low boredom threshold.'

'I imagine it's a family trait.' She drank some more of the juice. 'And if I decide to ignore your command?'

The amber eyes met hers starkly and sombrely. He said, 'Then I shall make you sorry—sorry that you ever came here.'

'You're too late, *signore*.' Lucy lifted her chin. 'I already regret it more than anything in my life. So, what have I got to lose?'

The silence between them seemed to stretch into eternity. She saw his face harden into a bronze mask. Watched him take one long stride towards her. And stop, as if he'd suddenly found himself on the brink of some abyss.

He said with remote civility, 'In that case, *signorina*, there is no more to be said.'

Then the door to the *salotto* opened and Fiammetta came in on a gale of laughing apologies, the children following in her wake.

Lucy went over to the window, staring unseeingly at the shadows falling across the garden.

She thought, So that's that. And wished with all her heart that she could feel relief instead of this aching wilderness of desolation.

CHAPTER EIGHT

IF LUCY hadn't been feeling so raw, dinner at the Villa Dante that evening would have been almost funny.

Philip, seated by the *contessa*, found all his conversational overtures either stonily blocked or sent whistling past his ear in the verbal equivalent of a passing shot, however much charm he exerted. Before the melon and prosciutto was finished, and the next course of chicken in a wine sauce served, he had developed a hunted look.

Angela, in a cream silk sheath which would probably have cost Lucy three months' salary, and did more than justice to her seductive cleavage and long, shapely legs, was focusing all her attention on Giulio. The lowered voice, the body language which virtually excluded everyone else at the table with one turn of her shoulder, the hand toying with his cuff button, the soft, breathy giggles—all these proclaimed a long-established and unassailable intimacy.

Which Giulio's own behaviour did nothing to contradict, Lucy admitted fairly and with pain. He was relaxed, the dark face amused and intent as he responded to his companion.

Lucy's forebodings, it seemed, had been perfectly justified. Philip, she addressed him silently, you haven't a prayer. So much for your romantic holiday. All this and the Uffizi too.

She concentrated her own efforts on persuading the children to sit still and eat, and lending an ear to Fiammetta's rapturous description of the apartment in

New York that they would all be moving into in the autumn.

She too would move, she decided. She might even change jobs when she got back to London. Make a whole fresh start. Seek forgetfulness and healing in a frenzy of activity and new horizons. And pray that it worked.

Marco nudged her. 'When does the day start?' he whispered conspiratorially. 'The day when we have to be good.'

'Right this minute,' she whispered back. 'Twenty-four whole hours. So no being horrid in the night.'

His crestfallen air suggested that plans for tormenting Emilia had been well advanced. Then, with a philosophical shrug, he applied himself to his peach ice cream.

It was when coffee was served and the carafes of grappa and Vin Santo appeared on the table that everything suddenly changed.

The *contessa*, ignoring Philip, was talking to Fiammetta, waving a languid hand as she made a point, when Giulio leaned forward.

'My dear Claudia.' His voice was silky. 'I see you are wearing the Falcone ring tonight. Does this mean you are returning it at last?'

The *contessa* glanced at her hand. The ring in question, Lucy saw, was a spectacular ruby in an antique gold setting.

'*Caro* Giulio,' she purred. 'How wicked of you to raise such a subject with strangers present. We surely do not need to—wash our linen in public.'

Giulio shrugged indifferently. 'My attempts to do so privately have been fruitless. As your lawyers have told you on several occasions, the ring is an heirloom, not a piece of costume jewellery, and should have been given back to the Falcone estate after my father's death.'

'In order that the new Conte Falcone might present it to his wife?' Claudia Falcone gave a silvery laugh.

'But you have no wife, *mio caro*. Indeed, you are becoming quite famous for remaining single.'

She lifted her shoulders in an elegant shrug. 'So—the matter is in your own hands.' Her smiling glance rested obliquely on Angela. 'All you have to do is gratify the wish of my heart by announcing your engagement, and I shall willingly bestow the ring on your bride to be.'

She stretched out her hand, studying the ruby at arm's length. It glowed like blood and fire on her thin finger.

'This is a tiresome argument,' Giulio Falcone said coldly. 'My marriage plans have no bearing on the issue. The ring belongs to the estate whether or not I stay a bachelor to the end of my days.'

'And is that what you intend?' Her arched brows lifted in challenge.

'No,' he said coolly. 'I shall be married before the year is out. But that—forgive me, my dear Claudia—is no concern of yours. And the presentation of the jewel to my *fidanzata* is also a private matter, not some ritual devised and orchestrated by you.'

'What a drama.' Claudia laughed again, but a tiny muscle twitched at the side of her mouth. 'We should apologise to our guests, *caro*, for subjecting them to this boring family squabble.' She looked at Giulio, her eyes hard, her lips thin. 'I cherish the ring in memory of your dear father. I cannot believe that you could be so heartless as to deprive me of it without just cause.'

'My cause is just,' Giulio returned icily. 'And established in law.'

Claudia inclined her head regally. 'And when you decide to marry I will hand it over. Until then, it is perfectly safe with me—indeed I hardly let it out of my sight—and there is no more to be said.'

Marco was still scraping the last of his ice cream from his plate, but Emilia's eyes, Lucy saw, were like saucers.

They should not, she thought grimly, be hearing all this. And nor, she added as anguish lanced through her, should I.

She pushed back her chair. 'With your permission, *signora*, I will put the children to bed. It's been a long day.'

'Twenty-four whole hours,' Marco contributed brightly, and a laugh ran round the table, visibly dissipating the tension.

'Come to me, *carissimo*.' The *contessa* held out her arms to the child, and he ran round the table to her, to be hugged and kissed. When it was Emilia's turn, Lucy noticed with fury, her grandmother simply touched a swift, indifferent hand to the child's cheek and immediately turned away.

'I will come with you.' Fiammetta helped Lucy usher the children from the dining room. '*Dio mio*, what a scene!' she confided in an undertone as they walked through the night-scented garden, the children scampering ahead. 'The problem is, the ring has great value—it dates from the fifteenth century—and it should be kept in the bank. Mamma knows this, but always she has some excuse not to hand it back, and now Giulio has become angry, and little wonder.'

She rolled her eyes to heaven. 'And so it is war between them. I only hope Mamma does not do something foolish. She is not good with money, you understand,' she added with an expressive shrug. 'If Giulio took her to court, as he might, she could be ruined.'

'Can't you—reason with her?' Lucy suggested awkwardly.

'Over some things, but not this. She will not listen. And she provokes him constantly, as she did tonight, by flaunting it on totally unimportant occasions.' She sighed. 'Perhaps he should not have said what he did, but I cannot blame him.'

'Maybe she was trying to needle him into proposing to your cousin there and then.' Lucy spoke haltingly, the words stabbing her like knives.

'Then she does not know Giulio,' said Fiammetta dismissively. 'Although it cannot be long,' she added, after a pause. 'Did you see how they were together tonight?'

'Yes,' Lucy said dully. 'I saw.'

'And this poor Philip Winslade, who has now served his purpose...' Fiammetta gave another gusty sigh. 'If I were in his shoes, I would not stay here to be humiliated any further, would you?'

'Perhaps he loves her,' Lucy said slowly. 'Maybe he's prepared to endure anything just to be with her, even if he knows, deep down, he's wasting his time—that all the future can promise him is pain and loneliness beyond belief.'

Fiammetta shot her an amazed look. 'Why, Lucia, that came from the heart, I think.'

And it's also given far too much away, thought Lucy, seeing the inevitable questions forming on her companion's lips.

She quickened her step. 'Slow down, you two,' she called. 'It's dark, and you're going to fall and hurt yourselves.'

Any hint of possible damage to her little ones was exactly the right diversion for Fiammetta, who fussed the remainder of the way to the *casetta*.

The children's bedtime passed without trouble, although Emilia was inclined to whinge and cling to her mother. But who could blame her for that? Lucy thought wearily.

When Fiammetta had departed for the villa, and the *casetta* was quiet, Lucy went and sat down on the stone bench outside the door. After the stillness of the day, the night was full of noise and movement—the rasping of crickets, the moths swooping round the overhead lamp, the harsh cry of a bird.

And, rising above the villa, there was the moon's golden crooked smile, which seemed in Lucy's present vulnerable state to be taunting her.

She had her book on her lap, but she didn't open it. Her mind was running riot with thoughts and impressions, most of them unhappy. How could your whole life—your whole perception of who you were and what you wanted—change so fast and so irrevocably? she asked herself, not for the first time. It wasn't sane—it wasn't rational.

Giulio Falcone had taken possession of her, heart, mind and soul. From that first encounter, she'd seen the danger—recognised what was happening to her—but been unable to resist.

Swept away helplessly, she thought, by the force of destiny. And who could tell where it would all end?

She rallied herself. Yet there'd been one positive step. She had kissed Emilia goodnight, and while the embrace hadn't been returned it hadn't been rejected either. Maybe if she could help stabilise the child, give her a sense of her own worth, then her stay in Tuscany would have some meaning—even some value.

The sound of approaching footsteps invaded her reverie, and she sat up sharply, her whole body tensing as a tall, familiar figure walked under the archway into the courtyard.

'Good evening once again, *signore*.' It took every scrap of courage she possessed to speak so nonchalantly. 'Have you come for another fight?'

'No.' His tone was dry, almost reflective. 'My battles are over for the day. I came to check on the children—and to make sure you have everything you need.' He paused. 'May I sit down?'

'Shouldn't you go back to your guests?'

'I invited Fiammetta and the children,' he said softly, 'and them alone. And as Fiammetta is playing cards, and the children, presumably, are asleep, I can now please myself.'

She moved to the far end of the bench, tucking the folds of her skirt around her. Giulio observed this manoeuvre with raised brows, then seated himself at the other end.

'You are not nervous, away from the main house?'

Not until this moment, she thought.

She said, 'I suppose you're going to tell me there are gangs of armed robbers roaming the neighbourhood.'

'No, thank God. Here we are among our own people.' He paused again. 'But down at the pool you mentioned that you thought someone was watching.'

She shrugged. 'Well, yes, but I could have been wrong.'

'Because it was not me, it follows that it must be no one?' There was an edge to his voice. *'Grazie.'*

'It might have been a cat,' she said lamely.

'Sì, or a wild boar, or a wolf from the hills.' His tone was exasperated.

'Or just my imagination,' she persisted. She managed a laugh. 'There's an old Chinese curse—May you live in interesting times. Well, I've lived through some fascinating ones lately. Perhaps it's made me a little paranoid.'

'I do not think you are that.' He was frowning. 'But I know you are unhappy, and it troubles me, because I am to blame.' He drew a breath. 'I never meant you to be hurt like this, Lucia, believe me.'

'Please.' All the breath in her body seemed to catch in her throat. 'I—I'd rather not discuss it.'

'But we cannot pretend that the situation does not exist.'

'You may not be able to,' she said almost savagely. 'But I can. I'm a great pretender.'

'Lucia.' He stretched a hand towards her, and she recoiled.

'No. Can't you see—don't you understand that talking about it only makes things worse? Can't you show me a little mercy at least?'

'*Dio mio,*' he whispered. 'I did not realise the wound had gone so deep.' The dark face was like stone. '*Columbina*—is there nothing I can do?'

'You said this morning that it would be better if I went.' She bunched her trembling hands into fists and hid them in the folds of her skirt. 'I—I've come to agree with you. I'll leave just as soon as you can find someone else to look after the children.'

He was silent for a moment, staring down at the rough cobbles. Then he said quietly, 'As you wish. Teresa has a cousin, training to be a teacher, who is looking for a vacation job. I will see what can be arranged.' He paused again. 'What will you do?'

'What I originally planned. Go back to England on the first available flight.' She moistened her dry lips with the tip of her tongue. 'Get on with my life.'

'How simple you make it sound.' Beneath the surface of the smooth words, something very different was bubbling. Something that could have been anger—even bitterness. 'How rational. And yet we both know it is nothing of the kind.'

Before she could guess what he was going to do, he had reached for her, the long arms drawing her roughly, inexorably towards him, lifting her so that she was lying across him, cradled on his thighs.

For a brief second, she saw his face above her in the moonlight, the suddenly harsh lines etched beside his mouth, the glitter in his eyes. The falcon, she thought dazedly, with his prey. About to swoop—to carry her off into eternal darkness.

Then his lips were on hers, fierce, searching, demanding a response which Lucy knew, in some distant, reeling corner of her mind, she should deny him. She knew she should struggle, beat him with her fists, make him let her go.

But the heat of his mouth and the scent of his skin were like some insidious drug, draining the power of resistance from her. Her head fell back helplessly against his arm as her lips parted in acceptance. Even welcome.

And when her hands lifted it was not in self-defence but to close on the whipcord strength of his shoulders and draw him down to her.

Because this was what she wanted, she thought achingly. What was the point in pretending otherwise? She could not have his love, or a share in his life, but she would take what little he could offer. A brief interlude of passion. A memory to warm her in the bleak emptiness of the future.

His mouth explored hers roughly, as if he too was driven by forces, needs he could not control. The thrust of his tongue was like burning silk, creating a sweet madness she had never known before. Awakening longings she had never realised existed.

She kissed him back, answering his fire with her own ardour, drinking him as eagerly as a flower absorbed the rain.

His hand went to her breast, outlining its rounded swell with fingers that shook slightly, before sliding with new mastery beneath the clinging top to push it upwards. To find and celebrate her warm nakedness.

For a long moment, he was still, cupping the soft weight in his palm. Then he took his mouth slowly from hers, his eyes studying her flushed face with telling awareness. As his gaze held hers, he began to move his thumb softly and rhythmically, circling—tantalising her nipple.

Lucy felt herself gasp in startled yearning. Saw him smile. Felt that smile brush her parted lips in a kiss of magical tenderness, before he feathered a caress across the delicate peak, bringing it to instant pulsating life.

He bent his dark head, his mouth seductive as it moved on her heated, tumescent flesh. The gentle tug of his lips, the faint graze of his teeth, the flick of his tongue on the hardened, sensitive bud—all these were a web of arousal enmeshing and enthralling her. As, somehow, she had always known they would be. As if she had been born for this moment alone, her body arched towards him in delight and an unspoken offering more eloquent than any words.

'*Mia bella, mia carissima.*' His voice was hushed, husky against her skin. He sounded, she thought, almost like a stranger. He lifted his head—looked at her. 'Do you know you taste of moonlight?'

Half-shyly, Lucy touched the dark, springy hair, then ran a hand down the column of his throat to the V of skin exposed by the open neck of his silk shirt. The need to touch him in her turn was overwhelming. Fingers shaking, she began to undo his shirt buttons. She spread her hands across his chest, savouring the texture of his hair-roughened skin, letting the race of his heartbeat thud against her palm.

She planted frantic little kisses over his torso, feeling the flat male nipples pucker and harden under the teasing of her lips.

He took her hands, kissed them and carried them to his body. 'This is how I want you.' The words were barely a whisper.

The breath caught in Lucy's throat as she recognised the strength and power that would soon be part of her— joined with her. She was aware of him parting the folds of her skirt, of the glide of his hand along her slender thigh, and her whole body clenched in anticipation and desire.

His mouth took hers again, but this time his kiss was subtle, sensuous, his tongue as light as a butterfly's wing as it explored the swollen softness of her lips, while with equal and unerring delicacy his long fingers began a more intimate quest.

Lucy sighed her acquiescence against his lips. Almost at once, she was caught, and drowning in a golden net of pleasure so acute that she wanted to laugh, to weep, to cry out all at the same moment.

But the scream that rang out was a very different one. It was a child's voice, shouting in fear.

The delight shattered in an instant.

'Oh, God.' Lucy tore herself, dry-mouthed, from his arms, pulling her clothing into place with frantic hands. 'Emilia! What's Marco doing to her?'

She flew into the *casetta*, taking the stairs two at a time, aware that Giulio was just behind her.

Emilia was sitting up in bed, her hands clasped over her ears, her face contorted, her mouth opening for another scream.

'Hush, darling.' Lucy knelt on the bed, drawing the child into her arms. 'What's the matter?'

She was engulfed in a flood of sobbing Italian.

But, whatever the problem, Marco could not be blamed, she noted thankfully. One glance at the other bed revealed him to be asleep and oblivious.

'She had a bad dream,' Giulio translated, sitting down on the opposite side of the bed. 'She was in a car that crashed, and she could not get out.'

'But that didn't happen, Emilia.' Gently, Lucy stroked the silky hair. 'You're here and perfectly safe.'

'Zio Giulio.' The child turned to him, still hiccuping with sobs.

'Lucia is right, *cara*.' Giulio took the damp bundle into his arms, and began to mop her face with his handkerchief. 'All is well.'

'Not Alison,' Emilia objected. 'She was hurt.'

'Yes,' he agreed. 'But even Alison will be well again soon. And to prove it I will take you to visit her. She has her leg in a big plaster cast, and she will let you draw a picture on it.'

'Really and truly?' The sobs died away as Emilia considered this new and entrancing prospect.

'Really and truly,' he confirmed, dropping a kiss on the top of her head. 'And now you must lie down and go to sleep again.'

'I want a drink,' Emilia decided fretfully. 'And for you to stay with me, Zio Giulio.'

'I'll heat some milk,' Lucy said quietly, and went downstairs.

Emilia's nightmare, she realised as she busied herself at the stove, had been her own salvation. Because she had been on the verge of giving herself, body and soul, to a man who belonged to someone else. A man who could only see her as a source of casual pleasure. And she would have been left to survive alone the pain and emotional battering of such a surrender.

Will I ever learn? she lashed herself mentally. Or am I simply stark raving mad?

But, thankfully, circumstances had restored her sanity without too much harm being done, except perhaps to her self-respect, she thought, recalling her enthralled, mindless response to Giulio's lovemaking.

She sank her teeth into her bottom lip as she poured the milk into a beaker, and carried it upstairs.

Emilia was calm enough, and even giggling a little at whatever Giulio was murmuring to her. She drank the milk without fuss, then settled back on her pillows, holding firmly onto her uncle's hand.

'And Lucia must stay too,' she decreed. 'Alison used to tell me stories. I like best the one about Cinderella.'

'So Cinderella it must be.' Giulio's eyes met Lucy's across the narrow bed. 'You know that story, *columbina*?'

I feel as if I'm living it, she thought, hurriedly looking away. Except that midnight has struck, I've changed back into my rags, and there's going to be no happy ending.

She felt absurdly self-conscious too, starkly aware of Giulio's presence, within touching distance of her. Indeed, the whole intimate scenario of the bedroom, the drowsy child, the two of them united in comforting her was almost too painful to be borne, encompassing, as it did, so many might-have-beens.

But there was still a kind of peace to be enjoyed in retelling the age-old story of love, loss and rediscovery, she found wonderingly. She kept her voice deliberately soft and even, and long before Cinderella had fled, leaving her glass slipper on the Prince's stairway, Emilia was asleep.

'She should be all right now.' Lucy got up gingerly. 'But I'll sleep with my door open, just in case.'

Giulio rose too, detaching his hand from the small fingers with infinite care.

'I think you are wasted on the advertising industry, *mia bella*.' The amber eyes studied her ironically as she paused on her way to the door to remove Marco's thumb from his mouth. 'You seem to have a gift with children.'

'Not particularly.' Lucy went out of the room and downstairs to the kitchen, head held rigidly high, aware that he was following. 'A story and a glass of milk doesn't turn me into Mary Poppins.'

His voice reached her quietly. 'Are you so certain you wish to leave?'

'More than ever.' Her reply was curt, and she kept her back turned as she rinsed the empty glass.

He said, 'You think if you stay, then I shall try to make love to you again.' He paused. 'I shall not. My behaviour tonight was a grave mistake. As things are, I had no right to touch you.'

'At least we agree on something,' she muttered.

'I have no excuse to offer,' he went on as if she hadn't spoken. 'Except that you were very lovely.'

And very willing. He didn't actually say the words aloud, but then, Lucy thought bitterly, he didn't have to. They were there just the same, quivering in the air between them.

Her tone was biting. 'And what excuse can I make? That you're clearly an expert in seduction, that I lost touch with reality for a few moments?'

'If that is what you wish to believe.' He sounded weary. 'At any rate, there will be no repetition. Is that the assurance you seek?'

She said raggedly, 'I don't want assurances, just my freedom.' She drew a harsh breath. 'And as soon as it can be arranged.'

'Then you shall have it,' he said almost savagely. 'And I hope for your sake, *carissima*, that it does not cost you too dear.'

She heard him go out. Heard the door close behind him. Realised she had been gripping the edge of the sink so tightly that her knuckles had turned white.

Slowly, painfully she unclenched her hands.

She thought, So this is where it ends. And I should be glad. But I'm not. Oh, dear God, I'm not.

And she felt one terrible dry, aching sob force its way from the tautness in her chest and explode, at last, in the relief of tears.

CHAPTER NINE

IT WAS a wretched, interminable night which Lucy spent tossing restlessly on her hard mattress.

She felt as if she was trapped in some terrible limbo. The thought of leaving—of never seeing Giulio again—was well-nigh unbearable. And yet she dared not stay either, because she knew that if she did she would be utterly destroyed.

Nor could she come to terms with how quickly this emotional devastation had invaded her life. How could all her expectations—her values—have been turned on their heads in little more than a matter of hours? And when, by rights, she should still have been grieving for Philip, too.

I must be terminally shallow, she thought in savage self-derision. But I don't even know who I am any more—or what's happened to me.

She'd viewed love as a stable commitment growing from mutual liking and shared interests, not as a tempest force of anguish, desire and jealousy, fuelled by an uncontrollable physical attraction, sweeping into her life, wrecking all her safe preconceptions.

That's not love, she argued silently. That's lust.

And perhaps it would die as swiftly and unpredictably as it had roared into life, overwhelming her almost before she was aware.

That, anyway, was all she could pray.

But her sleepless turmoil was not solely due to her troublous thoughts. Some of it at least was down to sheer sexual frustration, although it galled her to admit it. She had been aroused almost to the brink of fulfilment, lifted

117

to the heights, and then hurled into some dark abyss of pain and longing. She had been given a hint—a promise of passion's ecstasy. Now she needed the surcease of completion, of consummation.

But it was never going to happen, she told herself, biting her lip until she tasted fresh blood.

Her hands strayed down her feverish body, retracing the path his lips and fingers had taken. Her skin burned against the rasp of the thin sheet which covered her. She was molten with her need for him. Sick with shame at the temptations which racked her.

She turned over, burying her flushed face in the thin pillow. A temporary physical release wasn't what she needed. Only in Giulio's arms could the promise of love be satisfied. And nothing less would do.

It was nearly dawn before she finally drifted into a troubled sleep, and surely only five minutes later when a feeling that she was being bounced like a ball and a shrill 'Wake up, Lucia, I am hungry' from Marco dragged her back to full consciousness again.

He was kneeling on the end of her bed, testing its resilience with a series of energetic springs.

Lucy said wearily, 'Marco, this is not a trampoline. Go and get dressed, and I'll be right with you.'

'Have we been good? Has the twenty-four hours happened yet?'

She said crisply, 'No, you still have to do exactly what you're told.'

He was struggling into shorts and a T-shirt when she went into the children's room a few minutes later. Emilia, already dressed, was sitting on her bed reading. She sent Lucy a wary but not unfriendly look.

Which, Lucy thought, was a step in the right direction—or would be, perhaps, if she was staying...

Breakfast at the villa was a buffet affair. A selection of cold meats, cheeses, fruit, preserves and warm rolls was set out on the sideboard, with coffee and a tall frosted jug of freshly squeezed orange juice.

Lucy served the children, then helped herself to bread, cherry jam, and a pear.

She had barely sat down, when Angela arrived. She treated them all to an indifferent nod and walked to the sideboard. Without looking round, she said, 'My aunt wishes to have breakfast in her room. Will you see to her tray—er—Lucy, isn't it?'

For one dazed moment, Lucy surveyed the other girl's back, immaculately clad in white shorts and top, and wondered how it would look struck amidships by a torpedo loaded with cherry jam. Encountering a gleeful smile from Emilia, she realised that her feelings must be inscribed in capitals across her face, and hastily composed herself.

'Of course.' She paused. 'Miss—er—?'

'Brockhurst,' Angela supplied coldly as she came to the table. She gave Marco a look of distaste. 'Does he have to cram his mouth like that?'

Lucy, who'd been about to reprove Marco for the selfsame thing, shrugged instead. 'I like to see a child with a healthy appetite,' she tossed over her shoulder as she left the room.

Teresa supplied a tray laid with a snowy cloth, some special china decorated with a florid gold design, and a gleaming silver coffee service, and accompanied it with shrugs, grimaces and a commiserating pat on Lucy's shoulder.

As Lucy carried the tray towards the stairs, she was halted by Giulio's voice.

'What are you doing?'

Heart thudding, Lucy turned slowly. He was standing at the open front door, a dark silhouette against the morning sun.

Fighting to control her voice, she said, 'I'm taking the *contessa's* breakfast to her room.'

'On whose instructions?' He came a few steps closer.

For the first time in their brief acquaintance, he looked less than his usual impeccable self. He needed a shave, Lucy noted with a pang, and he seemed to have thrown on the clothes he was wearing the night before.

'Aunt Claudia's, darling.' Angela appeared from the dining room. 'Please don't hang around—er—Lucy. The *contessa* doesn't appreciate tepid coffee.'

'Nor does Miss Winters appreciate being treated like a servant.' There was ice in Giulio's voice. 'Your aunt has a maid to wait on her already. Where is she?'

'Probably pressing Aunt Claudia's clothes for the day.' Angela's eyes narrowed rather unattractively. 'Anyway, *caro*, what's the big deal? It's only a breakfast tray.'

'Of course it is.' Giulio took the tray from Lucy's unresisting hands. 'And as I am going upstairs I will take it to her myself. At the same time, I can clear up any misconceptions she may have about Lucia's role in this house.'

There was a jarring note in Angela's gurgle of laughter. 'Oh, I think we've all figured that out, my sweet.' She shrugged. 'But then, who am I to object to your little—escapades? I'm not immune myself.'

Lucy, stiffening with distaste, turned and went back to the dining room and her own tepid coffee.

But not before she heard Angela's stage whisper. 'However, if you're trying to make me jealous, darling, you'll have to do better than that pallid little stick.'

Which, Lucy thought forlornly, she supposed she deserved.

Clearly, it was going to be a very hot day. Lucy spent the first part of the morning trying to beguile the children into making a get-well card for Alison, but all they did was squabble over the design, so eventually she cut her losses and took them down to the pool for a swim.

Emilia was obviously nervous of the water, but trying not to show it, and Marco, from the safety of armbands, was inclined to crow over her, so Lucy found a ball in the small cabin where the loungers and mattresses were kept, and they splashed about happily in the shallow end, playing catch and piggy in the middle. Until...

'What a hideous noise,' Angela said acidly. She was standing on the edge of the pool, with Phiip hovering behind her looking ill at ease. She was wearing a black and gold swimsuit, with a matching silk jacket, and her feet were thrust into gold wedge-heeled sandals.

The wasp look, Lucy thought uncharitably.

'I've come here to relax,' Angela went on fretfully. 'Can't you take the brats somewhere else to play?'

Lucy said quietly. 'We've only just got here, Miss Brockhurst.'

'What difference does that make?' Angela adjusted the angle of her elegant straw hat. 'I'm telling you to go. I'd like some peace—and some privacy.' She flashed Philip a swift smile, loaded with meaning, then gave Lucy's chain-store bikini a contemptuous glance, without even changing gear.

'And I'm sure Zia Claudia doesn't allow the hired help to use the pool at the same time as her guests, anyway,' she added.

Controlling her anger, Lucy lifted the protesting children out of the water and wrapped them in towels.

She said, 'I'll try to remember that.'

'I should,' Angela said curtly. 'All my friends in England have nannies, and you wouldn't hold down a place for five minutes with your attitude.' She added in an undertone, 'And don't give yourself airs, my dear, just because Giulio may have made a pass at you. With him it's instinctive—a reflex action—and that's all.'

Lucy fastened her sarong around her with some de-liberation. In spite of her glamour and grooming, Angela, she decided with satisfaction, had heavy thighs.

'And which of us do you feel you need to convince, Miss Brockhurst?' she asked coolly, and, with a curt nod to the increasingly embarrassed Philip, marched the children away before the other girl could reply.

Both children were whingeing at full throttle by the time they reached the *casetta*, and Lucy could not blame them. She felt like whingeing herself when she saw who was waiting for them, tapping her foot in autocratic impatience.

'So here you are at last,' the *contessa* said with a snap. 'I wondered how much longer I would be kept here.'

'I'm sorry,' Lucy said woodenly. 'I didn't know you wanted to see me.'

'It is usual to present yourself to the mistress of the house for instructions each morning.' The hard eyes studied her. 'Are those intended to be working clothes?'

Lucy sighed inwardly. 'No, *contessa*, I was just going to change.'

'I am pleased to hear it.' The *contessa* paused. She herself was elegant in a mulberry dress and jacket, the Falcone ruby gleaming ostentatiously on her hand. 'I am going to lunch with some friends near Siena and I shall take Marco with me. Kindly see that he is properly and tidily dressed.'

'But Nonna—' Emilia's voice was woeful '—Zio Giulio said he would take us to see Alison in the clinic.'

'Your uncle has better things to do than attend to the wishes of a small girl,' the *contessa* said crushingly. She addressed Lucy. 'You will bring Marco to the villa as soon as he is ready. I wish to leave at once.'

Lucy said carefully, 'Only Marco?'

'You heard me, I think.' The *contessa* examined the enamel on her nails. 'My friends possess many valuable things, and Emilia, unfortunately, cannot be trusted. She had better remain here.'

'I do not want to go anyway.' Emilia's face was stormy. Lucy, placing a soothing hand on her small shoulder,

found that it was trembling. 'I hate you—hate you...'
Her voice broke down in sobs.

'What an outburst.' The *contessa's* voice was like drops
of cold water. 'And how dare you speak to me in such
a way? Are you sure you are equipped, *signorina*, to
deal with the problems of such a child?'

Lucy stood her ground, holding the weeping Emilia.
'Those of her own making, certainly,' she returned with
equal ice. 'As few of them are.'

'You are insolent.'

'No, just truthful.' She put a hand on Marco's
shoulder. 'Go indoors, *caro*, and wait for me,' she directed gently.

'I want to stay here.' He gave an excited jump, his eyes
going past her. 'Zio Giulio, come and see Lucia and
Nonna having a fight.'

'What is going on here?' Giulio came striding into the
courtyard, his amber eyes sweeping over them all. 'Why
is Emilia crying?'

'A storm in a teacup,' the *contessa* proclaimed dismissively. 'But I have to tell you, *caro* Giulio, that
Signorina Winters is not sufficiently mature to have the
care of these children. The example she sets is a poor
one. I demand you dismiss her instantly.'

'You are too late, Claudia.' Giulio's fine mouth curled
slightly. 'The *signorina* seems to share your view, and
offered her resignation yesterday evening.'

'Oh?' Claudia Falcone seemed startled. 'And who will
take her place?'

'Teresa's cousin, Dorotea, as soon as she can be contacted.' Giulio gently turned Emilia to face him. 'What
is it, little one?'

'Nonna said I was a thief.'

The *contessa* shrugged. 'I said merely that I was not
prepared to take her to the Masserinis for lunch until
her behaviour improves and she can be trusted.'

'Then you can have lunch with me instead, *cara*.' Giulio ran a finger down the child's tear-stained cheek. 'Go and wash and change.'

Emilia's smile was like the sun emerging from clouds, but the final glance she sent her grandmother as she went into the *casetta* was pregnant with malice. Marco trailed after her.

The *contessa* said, 'My dear Giulio, you cannot desert your guests in this way. Angela will be wondering what has become of you.'

'Then you will be able to tell her, Claudia—before you go to lunch with the Masserinis.' His meditative gaze went to his stepmother's hand. 'You are wearing the Falcone ring once again, I see.'

The *contessa* gave her tinkling laugh. 'But naturally, *caro*. Simonetta's jewellery is always so fabulous.'

His voice was too gentle. 'You think it appropriate to use a family heirloom, centuries old, to compete with that—that *arrivista*?'

Her mouth thinned. 'How dare you insult one of my friends?'

'You are mistaken. Simonetta Masserini is impossible to insult.' He paused. 'I request once more, Claudia, that you return the ring to me immediately. It is no longer your property.'

'And I repeat, dear Giulio, that I shall be happy to return it—but to your intended wife, and no other—as tradition demands.' She turned an arctic gaze on Lucy. 'Still here, *signorina*? You are supposed to be helping my grandson to change.'

'And I suggest you change too, Lucia.' There was amusement in Giulio's eyes, mingled with something deeper and more disturbing, as he looked her over. 'Firenze demands rather more formal dress, I think.'

He himself was wearing slim-fitting dark trousers and a plain white shirt, with the sheen of silk, unbuttoned at the neck, and with the sleeves turned back casually over his forearms. All traces of his earlier dishevelment had been removed, Lucy noted as she ran the tip of her tongue over her dry lips. 'You expect me to go with you?' she enquired uncertainly.

He shrugged. 'Naturally. Until your replacement arrives, you will carry out your duties in the usual way. And Emilia needs a companion in the car in case she is frightened or ill again.' He glanced at his watch. 'Will fifteen minutes give you enough time?'

Lucy nodded and whisked into the *casetta*. As she went upstairs to find the children she could hear the *contessa* obviously remonstrating with Giulio in furious Italian, and his cold, clipped responses.

The children were listening too, she discovered, and ushered them firmly away from the window and closed the shutters.

'They are quarrelling about the big red ring that Nonna wears,' Marco reported as Lucy hustled both of them into the shower.

'It does not belong to her. She should not have it,' Emilia said passionately as Lucy shampooed the chlorine out of her hair. 'I have heard Papà say so to Mamma—oh, so many times.'

'It's a private argument between grown-ups, and none of our business,' Lucy said firmly. 'Now, what are you going to wear?'

Emilia for once was no problem, dressing herself importantly in a brief red skirt and white blouse before shutting herself in Lucy's bedroom with the hairdryer.

However, it was a day's work to wrestle Marco into the velvet shorts and satin shirt which Lucy reckoned the *contessa* would deem suitable attire for the occasion.

'I hate these clothes,' he grumbled. 'But I like going to lunch with Nonna's friends,' he added slyly. 'They give me presents.'

'You get altogether too much,' Lucy said severely, combing his hair sleekly back from his forehead.

When they were both dressed, she sent them downstairs with picture books, and strict instructions not to get dirty—or quarrel—while she changed.

I'm playing with fire, she told herself as she changed hurriedly into a simple pale yellow shift, tying her hair back with a scarf of the same colour. But I don't care. I don't care about anything except that I'm going to be with him again—just for a while.

It was two incredibly sedate and tidy children that Lucy was able to conduct to the villa.

Fiammetta was in the *salotto*, flicking through a magazine, which she threw aside to embrace the children and adjure them to be good.

'And Lucia,' piped Marco. 'She must be good also.'

'*Sì.*' The ghost of a smile twinkled in Fiammetta's eyes. 'And Emilia will be there to make sure of it.' She extended a hand to Giulio. 'Have a care, *mio caro*. Sometimes, I think, you go too fast.'

'You have wisdom beyond your years.' The words and the kiss he dropped on her wrist were equally light, but the glance they exchanged was loaded with amused significance.

Lucy, noting it, frowned, then promptly relegated it to the back of her mind as the *contessa* swept in, imperiously demanding her grandson.

After Marco had been duly waved off with his grandmother, Giulio brought his own car round to the front of the house.

'Oh.' Lucy checked in surprise when she saw the sleek, low-slung saloon. 'But this isn't your car.'

'It is one of them,' he returned laconically. 'I thought it would be the most comfortable, as there are three of us.'

'I want to sit in the front,' declared Emilia.

'No, little one.' Giulio firmly strapped her into the back seat, in spite of her protests, then paused, his brows lifting, as Lucy got in beside her.

'What is this?'

She said quietly, 'I think I should be with her—in case, as you say, there's a problem.'

His mouth twisted. 'Are you sure you are not considering some problem of your own?'

'Quite sure.' Lucy gave him a straight look. 'I'm not the one having nightmares.'

There was a brief silence, then he said, 'Forgive me, Lucia. I should not have needed such a reminder.' He smiled at Emilia. 'You see, *cara*. You can pretend to be a great lady—a princess with your own *conducente*, and your lady-in-waiting beside you.'

'And where is my prince?' Emilia pouted a little.

'I think you may have to be patient for a while. But he will come one day, never doubt it.' Giulio swung himself lithely behind the wheel and started the engine.

'So, the day is ours,' he added, over his shoulder. '*Avanti*! Where shall we go, *principessa*?'

'To Firenze, Zio Giulio; you said so.'

'Ah, yes, but perhaps I've forgotten the way. You will have to give me directions, or we could end up in Rome. And you will have to speak loudly, because I'm old and growing deaf.'

Emilia giggled delightedly and sat up, peering out of the window, waiting eagerly for the first road sign.

There were sometimes muddles over which way was right and which left, and once the approach of a lorry rendered the child mute and visibly frightened, but, helped along by Lucy's soft-voiced interventions and encouragement, the game lasted cheerfully all the way to Florence.

'Thank you,' Lucy murmured to him as they left the car. He had parked in the middle of a vast square, dotted with bronze copies of Michelangelo's most famous statues, including the towering *David*. 'That was very kind of you.'

'And you think cruelty is more natural to me, perhaps?'

She was taken aback. 'Why—no.'

'*Grazie.*' He sounded faintly amused. 'Maybe I just wanted to avoid another reprimand,' he added silkily.

'Oh.' Feeling suddenly awkward, Lucy looked around at the rows of tourist buses disgorging their clients, at the vendors' stalls selling postcards and ceramics, and the inevitable ice-cream sellers. 'What is this place?'

'The Piazzale Michelangelo. The one place that everyone who comes to Firenze must visit, if they see nothing else. Look.' Threading a way between the pavement artists and watercolour sellers, he led her and Emilia to the balustraded wall.

Below them, bisected by the languid Arno, lay Florence, all pale stone and gleaming terracotta, her towers and domes gilded by the sunshine like some glorious medieval painting. And beyond, in the distance, rose the Tuscan hills, misted in shades of grey, blue and purple.

'It's almost too lovely,' Lucy whispered.

'*Sì.*' His voice was gentle, almost reflective. 'Lovelier than any dream.'

Lucy turned her head and found that he was watching her, his eyes fixed on her face. Instinctive colour flared in her cheeks, and she hurriedly transferred her attention back to the view.

'Whenever I have been away, this is always the first place I return to,' he went on, after a pause.

'Is that the Ponte Vecchio?' She craned her neck, feigning intense interest, trying to disguise her swift, burning awareness of his physical proximity, of his arm almost brushing hers on the stone of the balustrade, the hint of the expensive cologne she would always associate with him, and, more intimately, the unique male scent of his skin, warm and alive and tantalising her senses.

'Yes. It was the one bridge over the Arno left standing after the war. My father always said no one would ever know why the Germans spared it. As it is, many of the goldsmiths there have been able to hang up their signs without interruption since the time of Cosimo de' Medici.'

'Your ancestor,' Lucy said, straight-faced.

He laughed. 'One of them, perhaps.' He paused. 'You wish to buy something on the Ponte Vecchio—some trinket to remind you of Firenze?'

'I think I'll have to stick with rather cheaper souvenirs,' she said ruefully, and straightened, looking for Emilia, who had become bored, and wandered off to look at one of the exhibitions of paintings a few yards away. 'But I'll never forget this view as long as I live,' she added, conscious that she sounded like a polite schoolgirl. 'Thank you for showing it to me.'

He shrugged. 'Maybe this is my day for acts of kindness.' He straightened too, looking down at her, the amber eyes veiled by the sweep of his lashes. 'Yet I know very well I have not always been kind in my dealings with you, Lucia. And probably, in the end, I will have to be cruel—in order to be kind.'

His hand descended on her shoulder, swinging her suddenly and urgently towards him, and for one heart-stopping instant she felt the swift, bruising pressure of his mouth on hers, the shock of his body moulded frankly and demandingly against hers.

Then, with equal speed, before any of their fellow sightseers could register what was happening, she was free again, standing in the sunlight, a hand raised to her startled, throbbing lips, watching him walk away from her. Knowing that, one day soon, she would have to watch him walk away for ever.

And that, she thought numbly, would be the ultimate cruelty. But who could say she hadn't been warned?

CHAPTER TEN

By the time she caught up with Giulio and Emilia at the car, Lucy had steadied her hectic breathing, and managed to meet his sardonic gaze with a measure of composure.

'The little one is demanding ice cream,' he said. 'Perhaps we should have lunch before anything else. Do you agree?'

Without waiting for her reluctant nod, he swept them back into the car, and drove down into the city, eventually leaving the car in a quiet side-street off the Piazza della Signoria.

'Now we walk,' he ordained. He took Emilia's hand. 'We'll take the tourist trail for Lucia.'

He led the way briskly across the piazza, Emilia bouncing beside him.

'You recognise this?' he tossed over his shoulder.

Lucy was about to respond with a tart 'How could I?' when she realised that her surroundings were oddly familiar. She stared at the huge statues from Greek mythology, the commanding figure of yet another bronze *David*, the fountain, and the wide flight of stone steps leading up to an arched colonnade.

She laughed suddenly. 'Of course. *A Room with a View*. The scene where the young man was stabbed.' She halted. 'Have you seen it too?' she asked with surprise.

'In London, the year it came out.' Giulio paused too. 'It made me homesick.'

'And it convinced me I had to come here at all costs.'

'At all costs?' he repeated thoughtfully. 'Are you sure you have not already paid too highly for your journey?'

She said in a low voice, 'I'm not sure of anything any more.'

Giulio nodded, his face expressionless, and strode purposefully on.

Lucy found herself traversing a busy market, with crowded stalls selling table linen, souvenirs and Florence's famed leather goods. She wanted to linger, but Emilia seized her hand.

'Lucia, come and see Il Porcellino.'

Lucy found herself confronted by a bronze statue of a wild boar, his snout incredibly smooth and shining in contrast to the rest of him.

Giulio leaned down and spoke in her ear, his warm breath fanning her cheek. 'The legend says if you stroke his snout, *columbina*, you will come back to Firenze.'

Clearly it had been the ambition of a lot of people, Lucy thought drily, but it was hardly a safe one in her particular circumstances. Nevertheless, she lifted a reluctant hand and ran it over the gleaming metal, urged on by Emilia, who then demanded some coins from her uncle to drop from the boar's mouth into the grating below.

'That is good luck too,' she beamed.

'Good luck for the children's home which benefits from the money,' Giulio added.

'May I have some more money?' the child wheedled.

Giulio ruffled her hair. 'Later, little one. When we've eaten, I will bring you back.'

They ended up at a small restaurant in one of the narrow streets leading away from the Duomo, with pavement tables shaded by a dark green awning. A small, tubby man who was clearly the proprietor came bustling out to meet them, his face wreathed in smiles. He shook hands with Giulio, hugged Emilia ebulliently, with a promise that when she had eaten she would see the new litter of kittens in the courtyard at the rear, then turned a look of melting admiration on Lucy.

'*Bella donna,*' he breathed, disregarding Giulio's more laconic introduction. '*Bella donna.*'

They were shown almost reverently to the best table, and wine, mineral water and warm bread appeared instantly.

'Giovanni serves some of the best food in Firenze, and we're having the specialities of the house,' Giulio told her as a dish of *crostini* was brought—toasted bread spread thickly with rich, garlicky liver pâté. And this was followed by steaming platefuls of a stew made from thick chunks of sausage, haricot beans, sage and tomatoes. It smelled ambrosial, and tasted even better, as Lucy, who had planned to have a simple salad, soon discovered. She ate every mouthful. And afterwards there was tiramisu, thick and creamy and wickedly alcoholic.

'Food for the gods, eh?' Giulio smiled at her across the table, and forgetting she'd decided to be cool and distant, she smiled back.

'You must come here often to be treated so well.'

He shrugged. 'I live and work here, after all.' He poured some more wine into her glass. 'So, are you glad to be visiting Firenze?'

Lucy nodded. 'Naturally, I'd planned to come here.' She bit her lip. 'But I was overtaken by events.'

'As I was myself,' he reminded her silkily. 'But one visit is not enough. You must see more of my city before you leave.' He saw her lips curve involuntarily, and his brows lifted. 'Why do you smile?'

She shrugged. 'I live and work in London, but I'd never refer to it as *my* city.'

'Here in Tuscany, our sense of belonging runs very deep. For centuries men have fought and died for these same cities, whether as defenders or aggressors.' He drank some wine. 'And we Florentines like to win, sometimes at any cost.'

She looked at the careless strength of him, the firm lines of his mouth and chin, and could believe it.

She hurried into speech. 'The poet Dante was a Florentine, wasn't he?'

'*Sì*, and so was Beatrice, the girl he loved all his life. But Dante could not be content with poetry. He involved himself in politics, and was driven out of the city to Ravenna. There is a story in our family that he was given shelter in our home on his way into exile, which is why the present house bears his name even today.' He smiled at her. 'I like to think it is true.'

'Did he ever return to Florence?'

Giulio's face was suddenly sombre. 'No; he had too many enemies for that. But now, each year, on the anniversary of his death, the city sends oil to light the lamps on his tomb, so peace has been made with him at last.'

'I'm glad,' Lucy said softly. 'That's a nice story. Even if it does mean he never saw his Beatrice again.'

'Legend has it he only saw her once anyway,' Giulio said drily. 'As a young girl on her way to school. But she became his ideal, even though they both married other people.'

'That is silly.' Emilia, scraping the last vestige of ice cream from her dish, intervened. 'People who are in love should marry each other, don't you think, Zio Giulio?'

Giulio stroked her hair. 'It is not always possible, *cara*. Besides, although Dante loved Beatrice, she may not have returned his love. So perhaps it was better that he carried his passion in his heart only, and married for reasons of policy and sense.'

'I have finished all my food,' Emilia announced. 'May I go now and see the kittens?'

'Yes. I will join you when I have drunk my coffee.' He sent Lucy a faint smile, halting her instinctive protest. 'Relax, *columbina*. She will come to no harm. Enjoy some peace while you can.' He paused. 'Is it good to escape?'

'It's hardly that.' She tried to speak lightly. 'More a temporary reprieve.'

'And one which we all deserve.' The dark face was brooding, coldly introspective. 'Even Angela has the chance to be alone with her *amante*,' he added, with bite.

The sudden silence between them seemed to lengthen into pain.

Lucy found herself wondering if he had told her the story of Dante's hopeless love for Beatrice deliberately, as a warning of how quicky and how fatally love could strike. One glimpse and the young Alighieri had been lost for ever, without kisses or the promise of passion to fire his ardour either, she remembered.

And maybe Giulio wished to remind her too that she also could hope for nothing but heartache and endless yearning. And that hope itself was futile. Because Giulio's future was already mapped out for him for 'reasons of policy and sense'.

But I knew that already, she thought wearily. And it's far too late for any warning.

Before she could stop herself, she said huskily, 'Don't you—care about—that? About Angela's affair?'

'Yes.' His voice was grim. 'I find that this time I care very much.'

She swallowed. 'You—you could always put a stop to it,' she ventured.

You could ask Angela to marry you, she cried out to him in her heart. That would end her relationship with Philip in a flash, because she's only using him to make you jealous. Because she's greedy and ambitious, and he can't offer her what you can.

'I could,' he said. 'But it would solve nothing. What would be the point?'

Past the tightness in her throat, she said, 'When you—love someone...'

'Ah, love.' His voice was soft—mocking. 'That little dangerous word that can cover such a multitude of sins.'

He leaned forward, his amber eyes lambent, intent. 'How far should one go for love, I wonder, Lucia?'

She looked down at the table, tracing meaningless patterns with a fingertip on the white cloth. 'For the real thing, to the ends of the earth—to infinity,' she answered quietly.

'But is it right to love, and to go on loving someone when they have shown you plainly that they do not return that love? When they have hurt you quite deliberately—and very deeply too.' There was anger there, just below the surface, and anguish. Lucy heard them and winced.

'Maybe we can't control our emotions so easily,' she suggested with difficulty. 'Perhaps real love—the kind that lasts—doesn't allow any choice.'

'I hope,' he said grimly, 'that you are wrong.' He pushed his chair back and rose to his feet. 'And now I had better take Emilia to feed Il Porcellino again.'

'Not your usual lunchtime pursuit?' She was glad to change the subject, lighten the atmosphere.

'No.' He glanced at his watch. 'Normally at this time I would go back to my apartment for a brief *riposo*. A rest, *columbina*, in the cool and shade.' The amber eyes were hooded. 'Does the idea appeal to you?'

Her mouth felt dry. 'I suppose it's usual—in this kind of heat . . .'

'Quite usual.' A faint smile played round the corners of his mouth. 'And most enjoyable.' His voice sank huskily to a whisper as he leaned towards her across the table. 'Would you come with me, Lucia *mia*? Would you lie on my bed, in my arms, when the shutters are closed, and watch the sun make patterns on the ceiling?'

She was lost, whirling in the complex of emotions aroused by his words, in an agony of longing, of desire, that clenched her entire body, In that moment, she knew she would go anywhere—become anything he asked.

Then Emilia's shrill voice broke in impatiently, shattering the spell. Drawing her back from the brink of the abyss. 'Zio Giulio, Il Porcellino is waiting for us.'

Giulio sighed, briefly and harshly, then turned away, smiling at the child. 'And it would never do to make a wild boar impatient, of course. So, let us go.'

Lucy watched him walk away. She supposed she should be thankful that she'd not been required to answer. That Emilia had been there as an unwitting chaperon. Otherwise she could have put herself in Giulio Falcone's power for ever.

She shook herself mentally, glancing around her at the other tables, watching almost wistfully the people wandering past, many of them couples, their footsteps slow in the heavy midday heat.

The ever vigilant Giovanni, spotting her restlessness, appeared at her side. 'More coffee, *bella signorina*?'

She smiled and thanked him, told him haltingly how good the meal had been, and watched his delighted reaction.

'You tell Conte Falcone that next time he bring you for dinner I cook special meal. There will be candles, music.' He nodded vigorously. 'Very romantic.'

Lunch, Lucy thought ruefully as she sipped his hot, aromatic brew, had been quite perilous enough.

'*Ciao*, sweetheart. Have you escaped, or are you just out on parole?'

The drawled words brought her head round in shock. So this, she realised with irritation, was why she'd thought she was being watched. Hal, in brief shorts and with a shirt tied casually at the midriff, was standing beside her. The smile he gave her was frankly proprietorial. 'Mind if I join you?'

'Actually, yes.' Lucy reached for her bag. 'I was just leaving.'

'You keep telling me that,' he complained. 'You're not very friendly, are you?'

She shrugged. 'Perhaps I don't appreciate your brand of friendship.'

He laughed. 'You like it better Italian style?' He sat down. 'Nina was bug-eyed with jealousy that the handsome Count chose you out of all of them, but I told her you had hidden depths.' He paused. 'She hoped, when he showed up at Lussione, that he might have had a change of heart—or partner—but all he wanted was to ask a lot of questions about your background. She was spitting nails about it.'

Lucy frowned. 'Lussione?'

'Yes, he arrived yesterday morning just after breakfast, doing his magnifico act. Ben's parents were terribly impressed.' He laughed. 'I hope he was pleased with the reference Nina gave you. I wouldn't have been.'

Lucy could imagine. No wonder he thought she was such easy game, she thought bitterly.

She moistened her lips with the tip of her tongue. 'How are the others?' she asked quickly.

'The in-fighting has been spectacular. You never know who's with who, or for how long. I stay clear of it all.' He put out a hand and ran it down her bare arm. 'Having lost out on the one I wanted.'

His touch seemed to have left a trail of slime on her skin. Lucy wrenched her chair away to a safe distance as Giovanni materialised again.

'You wish to order, *signore?*'

'No, just exchange the time of day with the *signorina.*'

Giovanni stood his ground, his usually merry face unsmiling suddenly. 'This is my restaurant, *signore.* People come here to order food, and nothing else.'

'What the falcon has, he holds,' Hal remarked mockingly. 'Well, I can take a hint.' His smile lingered on Lucy's frozen face. 'If things don't work out with the Count—and rumour has it he loves them and leaves them in pretty short order—then you know where to find me.'

He bent towards her, and Lucy, sensing his intention, turned her head swiftly, so that his insolent kiss landed nearer her ear instead of on her mouth.

And she saw, over his shoulder, Giulio standing a few yards away, his face a bronze mask of hauteur.

'*Ciao*, baby.' Hal wore his triumph like a badge as he sauntered away.

'Your friend from the villa,' Giulio commented icily as he joined her.

'You both share a curious view of friendship.' Lucy was still shaking with temper.

'Is that all we share?' The question was so swift, so harsh, it was almost like a blow in the face.

Lucy felt the blood rush into her cheeks. She said sharply, 'Just what the hell are you implying? I wasn't aware there was anything to share.'

'Then you have a short memory, *mia bella*.' Giulio tossed the package he was carrying onto the table, nearly overturning a glass, and signalled imperiously to Giovanni for the bill.

'And so have you, apparently.' She glared at him. 'You can't imagine—even for a moment—that I wanted *that*.'

'I don't need imagination. I know what I saw.' His tone was harsh. 'For a woman who claims to be deeply, even painfully in love, Lucia, you bestow your kisses with astonishing ease.'

For a moment she stared at him, stunned, mute with outrage. How dared he level such an accusation, when he himself had quite cynically tried to seduce her? When the woman he planned to marry was conducting an affair under his own roof? Not only was he totally amoral, she decided in bitter disillusion, but an expert in double standards to boot. And how could she have allowed herself to forget that, even for a moment?

Mentally squaring her shoulders, she went recklesssly on the offensive. 'Think what you like, *signore*,' she flung at him. 'Believe whatever you were told at Lussione. I gather you went there to check up on me.'

His eyes narrowed. 'Among other things.'

'And decided I had just sufficient moral fibre to look after the children?' She glared at him. 'You, of course, being a fit judge in such matters.'

'I am the head of my family, Lucia.' He looked past her, and she saw his profile, sculpted in bronze, as proud and remote as a hawk's. 'And I will go to any lengths necessary to protect its well-being and reputation.'

She achieved a small, contemptuous laugh. 'Occupying the high ground, *signore*? You surprise me.'

'And you, *cara*, have never ceased to amaze me.' His voice had slowed to a drawl as he turned back to face her, the amber eyes like smouldering flames. 'I presume you have now decided that Lussione is the ideal place to find consolation for your wounded heart?'

The silken cruelty of the words was like a knife turning in her heart.

She said tonelessly, 'Why not? After all, I have to go somewhere when Dorotea takes over.' She paused. 'Have you any idea when that might be?'

'No,' he said icily. 'But believe me, *signorina*, you will be the first to know.'

She bit her lip. 'And while we're on the subject, did you forget Emilia, or simply abandon her somewhere?'

His mouth thinned. 'She is there.' He indicated a pavement stall. 'Choosing flowers for her mother.' He indicated the package on the table in its black and silver wrapping. 'As I, like a fool, chose this for you.'

Lucy's chair scraped across the pavement as she got to her feet. She said raggedly, 'A kiss-off present, Count Falcone? Something to remember you by, instead of a session of love in the afternoon?' She shook her head. 'If you're expecting me to curtsy, and whisper, *Grazie*, then you're doomed to disappointment. I want nothing from you—not now, not ever.'

'Have the goodness to lower your voice,' he advised coolly. 'We are attracting attention.'

A swift glance around told her that they were indeed the fascinated cynosure of all eyes in the vicinity.

Biting her lip, Lucy rallied. 'Don't tell me they're not used to it, *signore*. Most people here seem to conduct ordinary conversations at the tops of their voices.'

'But not usually with me.' His voice was satin edged with steel. 'Now we had better leave before Giovanni has a heart attack.' He paused. 'I presume you have seen enough of Firenze for one day?'

'More than enough,' Lucy flung back at him, and retreated to join Emilia at the flower stall.

'They are all so lovely,' she breathed. 'Would Mamma like these yellow flowers, do you think, or perhaps the tall pink ones?'

'Why not a mixed bunch?' Lucy suggested overbrightly, furiously aware that Giovanni was no longer looking nervous, but was rocking with laughter at something Giulio had said to him. A remark at her expense, no doubt, she thought, smouldering.

The flowers were paid for and wrapped elegantly in gilt-edged paper. Emlia insisted on carrying them back to the car, chattering nineteen to the dozen as she clung to her uncle's hand.

She continued to talk throughout the journey home, happily oblivious to the icy silence that prevailed elsewhere in the car.

When they reached the villa, Emilia wanted to rush in and present her flowers to her mother, but Giulio was firm. 'Mamma will be resting, and so should you, little one. Go with Lucia, and Teresa will put your flowers in water until later.'

Emilia pouted, but turned away with Lucy. As Giulio mounted the steps to the main door, it opened and Angela appeared. She was smiling and holding out both hands to him.

'Darling.' Her voice dripped reproach. 'Why didn't you tell me you were going to Firenze? I'd have gone with you. I simply must do some shopping at Ferragamo, and Pucci.'

'Next time, *cara*.' Giulio took her hands, raising first one then the other to his lips. He added something else in a laughing undertone, which Lucy, thankfully, was by that time too far away to hear, her head held high, her facial muscles feeling as if they'd been paralysed.

You still have a job to do, she told herself. Do it.

Once in the shaded bedroom at the *casetta*, Emilia made no further protest, and Lucy, moving softly round the room, picking up and folding her discarded clothes, could see she was fighting sleep. And not prepared to give in without a struggle, either.

'Tell me a story,' she demanded, drowsy but imperious.

Lucy sat down on the edge of her bed. 'What story shall it be?'

'Cinderella.'

'Again?' Lucy queried teasingly.

'Yes, because Cinderella becomes a *principessa*, as Zio Giulio says I shall.' There was a small silence. Then she said, 'Do you hope a prince will marry you, Lucia?'

'Most of the princes in England have other commitments,' Lucy said drily. 'I'd be content with a good man who loved me.'

'Zio Giulio is a good man. And today I saw him kiss you. Will you marry him now?'

Lucy gathered her suddenly reeling wits. 'People sometimes kiss each other for all kinds of reasons, Emilia. It doesn't necessarily mean they want to spend their lives together. Often, they're going to marry someone completely different.' She saw a sudden image of Angela, smiling triumphantly, complacently, and cleared her throat. 'Now—once upon a time...'

Emilia was asleep long before the story ended. Lucy went quietly down the stairs. She would sit in the corner

of the courtyard under the pergola and do some
sketching, she told herself. And she would not allow
herself to think, or wonder. Or to hope. Especially not
to hope.

The first thing she saw was the package in its black
and silver wrapping, lying in the middle of the living-
room table, a note slipped under the ribbon tie.

He must move as quietly as a cat, Lucy thought.
Because she'd not had the least inkling of his presence
downstairs.

Lucy unfolded the slip of paper and looked at the
words marching decisively across the page. 'Regard this,
please, as a gift without strings,' she read. 'Or even as
compensation. And believe that I want nothing in return.'

Impelled by curiosity, and something less easy to
define, Lucy tore off the wrapping paper and opened
the box inside. She unfolded the layers of tissue and,
hands shaking, drew out a handbag. On lines of classic
simplicity, it was made of the softest, most exquisite
leather, and the clasp was gold. For a moment, she stood
quietly, looking down at it, running a hand over it,
savouring the luxurious texture, the expensive scent of
the leather. Then she undid the clasp.

Inside, she found a plain white card. Across it was
written 'Giulio' and nothing else.

Aware of the thundering of her heart, Lucy lifted the
card swiftly and gently to her lips, then slipped it back
into one of the pockets in the rich silken lining.

A remembrance of him, she thought, that would
remain with her, bitter-sweet, for the rest of her life.

CHAPTER ELEVEN

IT WAS a very long afternoon. Despite all Lucy's gritted-teeth determination, her beloved drawing and painting failed to provide their usual anodyne effect. Whatever sketch she attempted, the image of Giulio's tall figure intruded somewhere, her fingers, it seemed, powerless to exclude him.

She had, of course, to thank him for the bag. The realisation hung over her like a cloud. Somehow she had to find words that would accept the gift in the spirit with which it had been given.

Whatever that was, she reminded herself ironically. She'd read his note a dozen times, but she was still none the wiser.

It was almost a relief when Marco returned, fretful with over-excitement, clutching the latest and most expensive model car with remote control. Emilia had just woken from her nap, and, seeing the sullen lines of her mouth as Marco exuberantly demonstrated his toy, Lucy diplomatically suggested that the car should be put away, and that both children do some painting instead.

They entered wholeheartedly into the project, and preventing them covering each other and the surrounding area in her precious watercolours kept Lucy fully occupied until it was time to order them indoors to change for dinner.

As they walked up to the villa, her mind seemed emptied of everything but the prospect of seeing Giulio— facing him again. She found herself silently rehearsing over and over again the polite, formal words of thanks which seemed safest. But the first person she encountered in the hall was Philip, his face like thunder.

'I'd like to know what the hell's going on,' he said savagely. 'I've just learned from that aunt of hers that Angela's going out for the evening with the Count. She's never said a damned word to me about it.'

'I'm sorry,' Lucy said levelly, directing the children to run on ahead of her to the *salotto* as she suppressed the involuntary pang his words had induced. 'But they're both free agents.' She bit her lip. 'After all, you and Angela aren't engaged, are you?'

'No,' he admitted sulkily. 'But we had an understanding—or so I thought, anyway. Now I'm not sure of anything. She's been a different girl since we arrived in Italy.'

I doubt it, Lucy thought drily. I think she's always been like this, and that now she's just not bothering to pretend any more.

'I don't know what to do for the best,' he went on fretfully. 'I've a good mind to clear out myself. Cut my losses and go back to England. What do you think?'

Lucy gave him a look of total disbelief. 'I think the decision has to be yours, Philip. I'm hardly the best person to advise you.'

'You're a woman,' he said impatiently. 'Would it bring her to her senses if I walked out on her?'

It certainly brought me to mine, Lucy thought wryly, but not in the way you mean.

She said quietly, 'I think that when you love someone you should stand your ground and fight for them, whatever pain it may cause you. I don't believe in giving up—in running away.'

'*Bravo*, Lucia.' A familiar voice, tinged with mockery, broke in as Giulio walked down the stairs towards them. His smile was taut as he surveyed her. 'I wonder if your courage will get the reward it deserves?'

The careful little speech—grateful without being grovelling, she'd assured herself—was immediately erased from her mind. For a fleeting instant, she allowed herself one devouring glance, absorbing the elegance of the light summer suit, sitting easily across his broad shoulders and unashamedly defining the narrow male hips and long legs. His shirt was pale cream, and the silk tie bold with colour.

Dressed to kill, she thought. And she should be glad she wasn't the intended victim. Should be—but wasn't...

She felt her lips twist crookedly, achingly. 'I wouldn't think so for a moment, Count Falcone,' she returned composedly. 'Now I must go and find the children.'

She had just reached the *salotto* when she heard Emilia's voice rising in a torrent of angry words to a scream.

'Oh, God.' Lucy flung open the door in time to see Emilia, tears pouring down her face, launch herself at the *contessa*, beating at her with her fists.

She started forward, but Giulio was there before her, striding ahead to seize the hysterical child and pull her away, holding her with firm hands.

'What is the meaning of this?' His voice was harsh. 'What happened?'

'My flowers.' Emilia's voice was thick with sobs. 'The flowers I bought for Mamma—*she* has thrown them away. I hate her—I hate her...'

'Hush, darling.' Lucy intervened swiftly, going down on one knee and putting a sheltering arm around the child's heaving shoulders. She gave the *contessa* a level look. 'I'm sure there must be some mistake. Your grandmother wouldn't deliberately destroy your mother's present.'

Claudia Falcone's painted mouth was set like a snare. She shrugged. 'I found this tasteless jumble of flowers in a bowl on that table. They were clearly dying so I disposed of them.'

'They weren't dying—they weren't...' Emilia lifted a tear-stained face from Lucy's shoulder. 'You're lying. You're wicked—a witch.'

'*Basta!* Enough.' Her uncle's voice silenced her. He turned to the *contessa*. 'You did this thing? Why?'

She sighed elaborately. 'I cannot bear to be in a room with wilting flowers—it is a foible of mine and—' a metallic note had crept into her voice '—surely a minor matter compared with the outburst of wild and violent temper to which I have been subjected. As you saw for yourself, *caro* Giulio, Emilia is clearly beyond control— maybe even unbalanced. Perhaps Fiammetta will believe me now when I say the child needs strict and disciplined supervision.'

She took a step forward, and Lucy felt Emilia shrink towards her.

'This nomadic life, following their parents from one city to another, is not the kind of stable existence that children need. How many times have I said it? And after this latest episode Fiammetta must and shall agree with me.'

Giulio was frowning, his expression withdrawn. 'Something will certainly have to be done,' he said, after a pause, his amber eyes resting expressionlessly on Emilia.

'You can't mean that.' The words seemed to burst from Lucy as the child flinched in her embrace. She looked up at Giulio in passionate appeal. 'Emilia shouldn't have behaved like that, but she was hurt and upset. And provoked,' she added hotly. 'Treating the flowers she chose for her mother like unwanted garbage was cruel—and heartless.'

There was a taut silence, then the *contessa* said, 'So Signorina Winters is now the arbiter of conduct in this house.' Her laugh jarred. 'We need not ask ourselves who has been encouraging Emilia to behave like some child from the gutter. The child attacks me violently, and the young woman to whom she has unwisely been entrusted makes excuses for her.'

Giulio's face was stern. He said quietly, 'Take the children back to the *casetta*, Lucia. I will ask Teresa to serve your meal there.'

Lucy scrambled to her feet, Emilia's hand trembling in hers. She said, '*Signore*—Giulio—please may I speak to you alone?'

He seemed to look through her. 'I regret that I have no time at present, *signorina*. We will speak tomorrow.'

'Then I'd like a private word with Signora Rinaldi.' Lucy stood her ground.

'Fiammetta is suffering from a severe headache. She will be dining in her room and does not wish to be disturbed.' He spoke with faint impatience, as if his mind was elsewhere. 'Now do as I ask, Lucia, *per favore.*'

As if on cue, Angela appeared in the doorway. '*Caro.*' Her voice dripped reproach. 'I'm waiting. We're wasting a beautiful evening.'

Her hair gleamed like black silk, and the vivid pink dress showed off her tan to perfection.

Lucy, with detachment, imagined her bald and with several front teeth missing as she shepherded her charges, one still sobbing, the other protesting hotly, to the door, and safely out of the room.

But not before she heard Giulio say, 'Forgive me, *mia cara*. I promise the remaining hours will be devoted solely to you.'

Not to mention the rest of his life, Lucy thought wearily as they all trudged silently back to the *casetta*. But if he was determined to tie himself to such a spoiled, manipulative bitch there was nothing more to be said. And for the sake of the Falcone bank she could only hope he had better judgement in financial matters then he did in his choice of wife.

'Why are you crying?' Marco demanded.

'I'm not,' Lucy denied, blinking hard.

'Zio Giulio will not take us on the picnic now,' he opined gloomily. 'And I have been good. It is just Emilia.'

Lucy sighed. 'That's unkind and unjust,' she said sternly. 'How would you like it if your grandmother threw away a present you'd bought?'

'She would not,' he said, unanswerably.

So sure of his position as the favoured child, Lucy thought sadly, unlike the sniffing waif walking at her other side.

She managed to persuade Emilia to eat some of the delicious food which Teresa, full of sighs and commiserating looks, brought down to them, and then diverted both children with games of picture snap and snakes and ladders until bedtime. She'd expected problems with Emilia, but the little girl was asleep almost as soon as her head touched the pillow.

Lucy herself felt restless and on edge. She washed up the supper things and piled them onto a tray, ready to return to the villa, then tidied away her paints, pencils and sketch blocks.

She played solitaire for a while, but found herself deadlocked after only a few moves in each game. How like life itself, she thought with irony as she shuffled the cards together and thrust them back into the pack.

She tried to read, but the story failed to hold her attention.

Almost as a last resort, she went to bed, but her attempts to sleep were futile. She found herself tossing restlessly on her pillow, her mind awake and all too alert, her imagination filled with images of Giulio and Angela, dining together on some moon-drenched terrace high in the hills, their voices hushed and intimate, his hand assured as it reached for hers across the table...their fingers clasped closely in promise...

'Oh, to hell with it,' Lucy said angrily, sitting up and pushing away the encircling sheet. 'Midnight or not, I'm going to wash my hair.'

In the past it had always worked as a kind of panacea. Now, standing under the cascading water, allowing her fingers to massage away the tension in her scalp, Lucy felt soothed and refreshed almost in spite of herself.

Changed into a clear white cotton nightshirt, she glanced in at the children to make sure they hadn't been disturbed, before going quietly downstairs in her bare feet. She put water on to boil for coffee, then unlatched the front door and wandered outside, wincing a little at the chill of the cobbles.

After the heat of the day, the night air felt still and strangely heavy, and, glancing up, she saw the moon, hazy and unsubstantial behind a mask of vapour.

A clouded moon, she thought, grimacing, as she unwound the towel she was wearing turban-fashion and began to rub vigorously at her damp hair. Storms ahead.

She paused, stiffening suddenly, as every instinct warned her that she wasn't alone. That one of the shadows in the corner of the courtyard was real and substantial, turning into the figure of a man, and coming towards her.

For a desperate instant, she asked herself what she was doing outside and defenceless. She opened her mouth to scream, and found that no sound would come.

Above the swift pounding of her heart, the roaring in her ears, his voice reached her, quietly and unmistakably. 'Lucia.'

'Giulio—oh, God.' Almost sick with relief, she slumped back onto the bench, her fist pressed to her lips. 'It's only you.'

'I must apologise.' He sat on the bench beside her, maintaining a careful distance between them. 'I seem always to be frightening you.'

And angering me, she thought. And bewildering me. And filling my heart with such ridiculous, overwhelming joy and delight that I don't know whether to laugh or cry. As in right now.

Aloud, she said sedately, 'Isn't it a little late for social calls?'

'It was not my intention to disturb you.' She could hear a slight undercurrent of anger in his voice, which instinct told her was not aimed at her but at himself. 'It did not occur to me that you would still be awake at such an hour. I—I could not sleep, and came out for a walk—to clear my head.'

'With me, it's hair-washing.' Lucy ran her fingers through the tangled, still damp strands, tossing them back over her shoulders, realising too late, when she heard him draw a quick, harsh breath and curtly turn his head away, that the action had clearly outlined her breasts under the thin cotton shirt, reminding her quite unequivocally that she was naked beneath it.

She said hurriedly, trying to conceal her dismay and embarrassment, 'I—I hope you had a pleasant evening.'

'It was all that I could have hoped for.' His silky tone gave little away. 'But I did not come here to discuss my social life.'

Lucy swallowed. 'No—you said you'd talk to me tomorrow—which it now is, I suppose.'

'But hardly the interview I had in mind.' He met her gaze again, a faint smile playing round his mouth, making her wish more than ever that she'd put on a robe—something that buttoned from throat to ankles.

'But we're here, all the same, and we may as well get it over with.' Lucy drew a quick breath, fighting for composure. 'If you wish me to apologise to the *contessa*, *signore*, I can't. I think her treatment of Emilia is a disgrace, and I always will.'

'Fortunately, it will soon no longer be your concern.'

She bit her lip. 'No—but you can't believe it would be good for her to be sent away to some ghastly school?'

'Whatever I think, the final decision must be left to Fiammetta and Sergio.'

'Over whom you naturally have no influence.' Lucy's tone was crisp.

'Not as much as Claudia has over Fiammetta.' Giulio pushed the hair back from his forehead in a weary, irritable gesture. 'And Emilia does not aid her own cause by clashing with her grandmother—whatever the provocation,' he added swiftly as Lucy's lips parted indignantly.

'If you really wish to help the child,' he went on, 'then keep her away from Claudia—make sure there are no more confrontations—between any of you. My stepmother makes a vindictive enemy.'

'I think I'd managed to work that out for myself.' Lucy's voice was subdued. 'I suppose leaping to Emilia's defence was about the worst thing I could have done.'

'Without a doubt.' He gave a quick, sharp sigh. 'When I asked you to look after the children, I had no idea there would be all these difficulties—these added complications.'

'Or you'd have thought twice about it,' she said quietly.

'Yes.' He sounded as if he'd been goaded into the admission. 'But at the time, Lucia, it seemed the only possible way. How could I have known that it would all go so terribly wrong?'

She said haltingly, 'You mustn't blame yourself— really. After all, everything's working out for the best...'

He drew a harsh breath. 'You can truly believe that?' he demanded. 'In spite of everything?'

'I have to believe it.' Lucy got to her feet. 'I don't have a choice.' She turned determinedly towards the door of the *casetta*. 'Goodnight, *signore*.'

'Wait.' His voice halted her. 'I want to tell myself,' he said savagely, 'that you will be happy.'

One day, she thought, when I've managed to cut you out of my heart, and erase you from my mind, I shall manage a measure of content. But never more than that. Because I can never be happy without you. I feel as if I've been shown paradise, then told I'll always live in outer darkness. But at least I've had that one glimpse. So many people can't even comfort themselves with that.

She smiled at him, lifting her chin. 'I'll be fine. And now you really must go. It's so late...'

'Yes,' he said. 'Too late for us both.'

She took a step backwards into the lamplit room, and he followed, as, somehow, she had known he would from the beginning of some distant time.

He closed the door behind him and leaned back against it, his hands spread against the timbers, as if he was keeping in touch with some last remnant of sanity and dared not let go.

His eyes met hers. Held them. He said very quietly, 'I want to see you, Lucia. Just this once—will you show yourself to me? So that I have it to remember—when you are gone?'

For a long moment, she looked back at him, letting the torment in his amber gaze, the shaken yearning in his voice blind and deafen her to the dictates of reason.

She was trembling inside, but her hands were steady as she began slowly and deliberately to undo the twelve tiny buttons which fastened her shirt. When the last one had been dealt with, she shrugged the garment from her shoulders, letting it pool at her feet. She stood naked in the lamplight, an offering of rose and pearl, dazzled by the flame in his eyes.

He was totally still as he looked at her, only the convulsive movement of a muscle in his taut throat betraying his tension.

She said his name once, softly, pleadingly.

And saw him shake his head, a slow, reluctant movement as if he was in pain.

He said softly, 'I cannot come to you, *mia cara*. I cannot kiss you or touch you because I dare not. Because if I did I would take you, and we both know that is not possible. Not now. Not ever.

'All I can promise is that I shall never forget this moment. That I shall always be thankful I can carry this picture of you in my soul.'

He turned and went from her.

For a while, she remained where she was, then, shivering slightly, she bent stiffly to retrieve her shirt from the floor and wrap it protectively round her body.

'And I shall remember too,' she whispered into the silence. 'I shall remember the sound of the door closing behind you—finally and for ever.'

CHAPTER TWELVE

LUCY was woken from a restless sleep by an unusual sound—the persistent splashing of water. For a moment, she thought she might have left the shower running the previous night, but, as she scrambled out of bed to check, the cool grey light permeating the room through the shutters told a different story.

The clouded moon had fulfilled its gloomy promise, and a curtain of rain was sweeping the hills, hiding the landscape behind a dank, impenetrable curtain.

The change in the weather had made the children peevish and uncooperative, she soon discovered, when she went in to get them washed and dressed.

'No picnic today,' grumbled Marco.

They were halfway to the villa, under the shelter of an ancient black umbrella which she'd found slumped like a dead crow in the corner of the living room, before Lucy had time to worry about coming face to face with Giulio again in what was literally the cold light of day.

The remembrance of their parting last night was an agony to her. She had offered herself, and been rejected, not because she was undesirable—the burning look in his eyes, every taut line of his body had told her differently—but for purely practical reasons.

His course in life was set. He was going to marry Angela, and Lucy was an inconvenient diversion, nothing more.

At least he had never tried to deceive her about his intentions, she thought, with an inward grimace. She didn't have to bear the humiliation of being used and discarded in a casual holiday affair—which was what she might have been offered if Angela had not suddenly arrived at the villa.

On the face of it, Angela might not seem the ideal wife, but at least Giulio had no illusions about her. She was from his background, approved by his family, and clearly they were both able to shrug off each other's pre-marital peccadilloes. It would be a pragmatic marriage, and who could say it would not work better than a re-lationship born of a sudden conflagration of passion?

But there was to be no immediate confrontation be-tween them. As Lucy was bracing herself to shepherd the children into the dining room, Fiammetta appeared wanly in the door of the *salotto*, indicating that she wanted a private word.

'I hear there has been a problem with Emilia,' she said unhappily, closing the door behind them.

'Emilia had a problem, certainly,' Lucy returned evenly. 'The present she bought you in Firenze was de-stroyed. She was very upset.'

'And my mother is—oh, so angry.' Fiammetta sighed. 'She says that Emilia is out of control—on the path to delinquency.'

Lucy bit her lip. 'I'm sure that's an exaggeration.'

'Well, I do not know what to believe.' Fiammetta's tone had become pettish. 'Sometimes I think Mamma is right and Emilia does need the discipline of a strict school.' She sighed again. 'If only Sergio were here. He would know what to do.'

Amen to that, thought Lucy. Aloud she said per-suasively, 'Then why not postpone any decision until his return? I'm sure the *contessa* couldn't object to that.' And, seeing that Fiammetta did not look entirely con-vinced, she went on, 'In the meantime, I'll try and keep Emilia apart from your mother.' She paused. 'She and Marco like to play with Teresa's children down at the vineyard, so we'll spend more time there.'

'*Cara* Lucia.' Fiammetta gave her a weak smile. 'What should I do without you? Especially now that Giulio has gone back to Firenze.'

Lucy was on her way to the door, but that stopped her in her tracks. 'Gone?' Her voice sounded wooden. 'I didn't realise...'

'Very early this morning,' Fiammetta confirmed. She sighed. 'He is such a comfort to me that I sometimes forget he has his work—his own life.'

Lucy had herself firmly under control. She said, 'But surely he'll come back in the evenings?'

Fiammetta shook her head. 'He does not usually spend time here during this season,' she explained. 'He came only for me—because there was a crisis. Now he probably will not return until September—for the vintage.'

'I—see.' Lucy swallowed. 'I thought that as Angela—Miss Brockhurst—was here he might make an exception to the rule.'

'I think Angela will be joining him in Firenze.' Fiammetta paused. 'Which leaves us with the problem of her guest. So embarrassing.' Her glance was suddenly speculative. 'It has seemed to us that he takes an interest in you, Lucia.'

Lucy forced an answering smile. 'Most unlikely.' Oh, dear God, if you only knew, she thought.

'But why not?' Fiammetta spread her hands. 'He is young and quite attractive.'

And it would provide a neat solution to the current difficulty, Lucy silently supplied.

She said pleasantly, 'I'm not looking for romance, *signora*. I'm a relief nanny, that's all.' She paused. 'Is there any word of Dorotea—when she can take up her duties?'

Fiammetta sighed again. 'It seems she is taking a vacation and cannot be contacted immediately. So vexing, when you too, Lucia, must wish to get on with your life. After all, you cannot always have been a nanny.' The pansy eyes were suddenly shrewd, and Lucy felt faint colour steal into her face.

She said, 'I shall just have to be patient for a little while longer. Now, I'd better go and see to the children.'

'You will have the house to yourself today.' Fiammetta examined the immaculate enamel on her nails. 'I am going to the clinic for a check-up, and Mamma accompanies me.' She glanced towards the window. 'I am sorry the weather is poor. What will you do?'

'I expect I can keep them amused,' Lucy said with spurious brightness, and went off to the dining room.

The children were in their seats, bickering loudly, while, at the other end of the table, Angela and Philip were engaged in a low-voiced but clearly furious altercation.

As Lucy hesitated in the doorway, Angela jumped to her feet and pushed past her rudely, muttering something in which 'like living in a zoo' were the only discernible words.

Philip rose also, watching her go. He gave Lucy a grim smile. 'Welcome to another lousy day in paradise.'

Lucy felt a flicker of compassion for him as she hushed the children and helped herself to some ham and cheese. If he really cared for Angela, he must be feeling totally gutted, she thought as she sat down.

She said quietly, 'I suppose you'll be going home.'

He shook his head, sliding into the seat next to her. 'Wrong. This is my holiday, and I'm going to enjoy it.' He gave Lucy a sideways look and his voice lowered intimately. 'I thought I'd drive over to Lucca. Fancy coming with me?'

'Thank you,' Lucy said evenly, 'but it wouldn't really appeal to the children, and Emilia's not a very good traveller anyway.'

'I didn't suggest taking them. Hand them back to their mother and give yourself a break. Let's face it, Luce,

we're both about as popular as a boil on the nose. And
you don't owe these people a thing.'

'I gave my word,' she said shortly. 'I'm not going to
break it.'

Philip shrugged. 'Please yourself.' To her relief, he
pushed back his chair and rose to his feet. He smiled
down at her, exercising his own brand of boyish charm.
'I can wait.'

Then don't stand still, Lucy thought as he left the
room. Because moss might grow on you.

In spite of her inner turmoil, Lucy found the day passing
much more quickly and pleasantly than she could have
hoped. And having the house to themselves was a bonus.

They had another painting session, then the children
made a batch of small sweet almond cakes under Teresa's
indulgent supervision. And the proceedings were rounded
off by a prolonged and noisy game of hide-and-seek.

Marco was always easily found, giving himself away
by shrill giggles of excitement, but Emilia was a far more
difficult quarry, thought Lucy as she left Marco in the
salotto happily playing with his new car while she re-
sumed the quest for his sister.

She had just reached the top of the stairs when she
saw Emilia coming along the gallery towards her, carrying something carefully in her hand.

'Lucia—see.' Her voice was censorious. 'Nonna has
left Zio Giulio's beautiful ring on her dressing table. A
robber might have stolen it. I shall give it to him when
he comes so he can keep it safe.'

Lucy gave the crimson fire of the ruby an appalled
look. 'What were you doing in your grandmother's
room?'

'Hiding,' Emilia said simply. 'But you did not find
me, so I won.'

Lucy groaned inwardly. Why the hell hadn't she declared the *contessa's* room strictly out of bounds? she

berated herself. Without knowing it, Emilia had supplied her grandmother with all the ammunition she needed.

She said gently, 'I think the best thing would be to put the ring back at once.'

'No.' Emilia clutched it firmly. 'I shall give it to Zio Giulio.'

'He's in Firenze.'

'Then I shall take care of it for him until he comes.' Emilia's expression was mulish. 'He does not want Nonna to have it anyway.'

'That,' Lucy said grimly, 'is not our concern. And your uncle will not be coming back—at least not for the foreseeable future,' she added.

'What is that?' Emilia frowned.

'A very long time.' Lucy held out her hand. 'No arguments, Emilia. I'm going to put that ring back where you found it. Your grandmother would be very angry if she knew what you'd done, or that you'd been in her room at all.'

'I do not care. I hate her.'

Lucy bit her lip. 'But she would also be very cross with me for allowing you to do it, and she would send me away. Is that what you want?'

Emilia considered her doubtfully. 'Would she truly do this thing?'

'Undoubtedly,' Lucy said briskly. 'Now give me the ring, and we'll pretend this never happened.'

The *contessa's* room was untidy, with clothes spilling out of the wardrobe and draped over the bed. The sour-faced maid was in no hurry to get on with her work, thought Lucy as she picked her way through the various pairs of shoes littering the carpet.

The ring glowed in her hand like a living flame. The temptation to slide it onto her finger, to see for one brief instant how it would look—how it would feel to be the chosen bride of the Falcone—was almost overwhelming. But that kind of dreaming was dangerous, so all Lucy did was deposit the ring among the general clutter of jars and bottles on the dressing table.

The air smelt cloyingly of Claudia Falcone's perfume. Lucy half expected to turn and find the *contessa* standing at her shoulder.

Feeling horridly like an intruader, she emerged, closing the door behind her, and hearing the sound echo along the gallery.

Another secret, she thought unhappily as she went downstairs, to add to all the others that must never be spoken.

It was very still, and very hot. Lucy, perched on a large rock on the hill above the vineyard, tested the wash on her painting, then began carefully to block in the jumble of faded terracotta roofs below her.

In the past week, the vineyard had become a sanctuary for herself as well as the children. Since Giulio's departure, the *contessa* had not bothered to disguise her animosity. Conversation at mealtimes was now conducted exclusively in Italian, and usually *sotto voce*, thus excluding Lucy on both counts. And Fiammetta's embarrassed efforts to remedy the situation had proved totally ineffectual.

Angela, who spent every day in Florence, though not, as far as Lucy was aware, any of her nights—at least, not yet, she qualified painfully—wore an air of glinting triumph that was almost tangible.

And, worst of all, Philip had quite openly transferred his attentions to Lucy, taking the adjoining seat at the dining table, making excuses to come down to the *casetta*, turning up at the pool when she was swimming with the children.

He was all smiles, confidential murmurs and admiring looks, apparently undeterred by oblique hints, studied indifference, even downright hostility, all of which Lucy had tried in turn.

With Fiammetta's well-meaning encouragement, he was constantly inviting Lucy to go sightseeing with him, or to drive out to dinner in the evening, and if he'd been anyone else, she acknowledged with a sigh, she might have been tempted, just for the chance of escaping the Villa Dante for a few hours.

As it was, she persevered with her stony rejections of his advances. And, as he hadn't seemed to have found his way to the vineyard, that was where she opted to pass her time.

Franco and Teresa's comfortable house, teeming with children and animals, fragrant with cooking smells, had become a second home for her, the language barrier easily overcome with Marco and Emilia's eager assistance as translators.

Teresa was the soul of discretion, but Lucy had noticed how her merry eyes clouded when the *contessa's* name was mentioned. It was clear that she cooked at the villa for the sake of Count Giulio, the beloved *padrone*, and no one else.

Lucy was fascinated by the day-to-day workings of the vineyard, laboriously explained by Franco. The big modern *cantina* with the vast concrete vats where the grapes were stored after picking, before being transferred to stainless-steel casks, was impressive, but she preferred the old *cantina* with its ancient oak casks and the dry, musty air redolent of generations of vintages.

Walking between the terraces of vines which lined the valley, feeling the rough ground under her feet, the sun on her back, made her feel closer to Giulio in some indefinable way, even if she knew in her heart it was only wishful thinking, and that, in reality, she was only setting herself up for more heartbreak.

Because he was far away in Florence, a remote figure in a dark suit, conducting formal meetings, enshrined in a glittering cage of high finance which she could barely comprehend. Occupying a different world from her own, just as he always had. And always would. And she'd been all kinds of a fool to indulge in the dangerous dream that their worlds could somehow touch.

She was suddenly aware of movement behind her, the scrape of a shoe on the rough incline, a shadow falling across the painting clipped onto her easel. For one sickening instant, she thought that Philip had finally managed to trace her to her refuge, and froze.

'Lucia.' Her name was spoken quietly by the last voice in the world she was expecting to hear. Her hand jerked, sending a trail of terracotta droplets across her picture.

He swore softly, dropping to one knee beside her, his frowning gaze assessing the damage. 'I did not mean to startle you.' He sounded shaken. 'But I did not expect to find you here either.'

'I come here most days.' Lucy forced control on her quivering senses.

'Alone?' His frown deepened.

'Usually I bring the children.' Her tone was stilted. 'But today they've gone to the clinic with Fiammetta to visit Alison. So I thought I'd catch up on some painting while I had the chance.'

'And I have ruined it.' He sighed briefly and harshly. He got to his feet, dusting the knees of his trousers. 'I am sorry, Lucia. You have real talent.'

'Thank you.' She hesitated. 'I didn't know—I mean— no one said you were returning today...'

He shrugged. 'No one knew. It was an impulse on my part. I had some free time, so I thought I would take the children on the picnic I promised.'

'Oh.' Lucy caught her breath. 'I thought you'd forgotten about that.'

Giulio shook his head. 'You will find, *columbina*, that I forget very little.' His voice was reflective, his gaze lingering openly on the deep unbuttoned V at the neck of her shirt, and the length of slim brown leg revealed by her brief shorts.

Aware that her colour had risen, Lucy said hurriedly, 'They'll be so disappointed.'

'I think they will,' he agreed. 'Especially as it is unlikely I shall have another opportunity.'

He must mean his engagement to Angela was announced, Lucy supposed unhappily. The other girl had never concealed her indifference to the children, and certainly wasn't the type to enjoy the rough and tumble of al fresco eating in some field.

She said quietly, 'What a shame.'

He shrugged again. 'So much for impulses,' he drawled. There was a pause. 'So, who is at the villa?'

'No one. Your stepmother and Miss Brockhurst have gone shopping, I think. But they'll all be back for dinner.'

'But I, alas, shall not. I have to return to Firenze.' He paused. 'You did not choose to accompany Fiammetta?'

'She asked me. But I thought she might like to be alone with the children for once. That it would be good for all of them.'

'And so you came to paint alone.' There was an odd note in his voice. 'A picture which I have ruined.'

'Maybe not.' She considered the painting, head on one side. 'Perhaps I can turn the spatters into birds or butterflies. It might even be an improvement.'

'You are very forgiving—and also an optimist,' he said drily. 'But leave your improvements until later.' His hand was under her arm suddenly, lifting her to her feet. 'Now you have a picnic to eat.' Sensing her hesitation, he added, 'You cannot leave me with a hamper of food and no one to share it with, Lucia.'

She should resist and she knew it. She should shun this exquisite forbidden pleasure, so unexpectedly offered.

A few hours alone with him, she thought yearningly. Their first shared meal alone since that night at the villa when he'd cooked her an omelette. Her heart soared and sang, and she knew she would not refuse him. That she could not.

She said sedately, 'Very well.'

CHAPTER THIRTEEN

APART from the whisper of the engine, it was silent in
the car. The breeze from the open window lifted tendrils
of Lucy's hair away from her face, and soothed her
heated skin.

She could still hardly believe she was doing this.

She'd assumed Giulio intended to stage the picnic in
a secluded corner of the villa's grounds. Instead, she was
seated beside him, being driven down some unfamiliar
narrow road which appeared to be leading nowhere.

'Patience.' There was a note of laughter in his voice,
indicating that he'd sensed her inner restiveness and was
amused by it.

'I feel I should have left a message at the villa.' Lucy
bit her lip. 'If Fiammetta comes back early with the
children, she'll wonder where I am.'

'Is she your only concern?'

'Not entirely.' Lucy could visualise the *contessa's* reaction if she ever discovered that the temporary nanny
was cavorting round the countryside with her stepson.

She heard Giulio sigh almost impatiently. 'Do you wish
you had not come with me?'

'No.' Her mouth felt suddenly dry. Her hands were
gripped tightly together in her lap. 'It's very kind of you.'

'The kindness, as ever, is yours, Lucia.' He sounded
suddenly remote, and her swift, sideways glance revealed that he was frowning again. Perhaps, she thought,
he was having second thoughts about the expedition.

She tried to think of some way to bring Angela and
his commitment to her subtly into the conversation—to
assure him that he did not have to worry. That she had

165

no intention of reading too much into this unexpected treat. But she knew it was impossible.

Best to keep quiet and enjoy herself for as long as it lasted, she thought. A memory to store away and cherish during the bleak times ahead.

She came out of her reverie with a start as Giulio swung the car off the road and parked it in the shelter of a tree.

'Now we walk.' He took a picnic basket from the boot of the car, handing Lucy a rug. He led the way through a timbered gate and down a track winding its way through a grove of ancient olive trees, their leaves shining silver in the sun. Somewhere ahead of her, Lucy could see the glimmer of water, and hear a faint, muted roar.

When they emerged from the trees, she stopped, her lips parting in a gasp of pure pleasure. They were on the bank of a small river, its waters cascading over a series of steep rocks before emptying almost vertically into a deep pool.

'Do you like it?' Giulio was smiling at her.

'It's wonderful.' She cast a worried look around her. 'But should we be here? It looks like someone's private land.'

'It is.' His face was straight, but the note of amusement danced in his voice again.

'Of course.' Lucy sighed. 'I'm an idiot. It's part of your estate. Do you own the whole of Tuscany by any chance?'

'Only in my dreams,' he returned drily. 'In reality, my property is quite small compared to others.'

And I, Lucy reminded herself ruefully, own a one-bedroomed flat with a window box. Way down on the relative scale of property values.

She did not want to contemplate the chasm of wealth or the centuries of history which divided them, so she busied herself with spreading the rug and unpacking the food from the basket. It was a varied selection, ranging from quail's eggs, a whole boned chicken stuffed with pâté and ham, salads in rich and subtle dressings and tiny savoury pastries to more homely slices of pizza, intended, Lucy guessed for the children. For dessert, there were peaches and grapes, and there was a bottle of dry, sparkling wine which Giulio cooled in the river.

She said shyly, deeply aware of his nearness beside her, 'You've been to a great deal of trouble.'

'More than you know, Lucia.' He was cutting deft slices from the chicken and putting them on her plate. 'You see, I did not come back solely to see the children but to bring some good news.'

She thought, He's going to tell me that he's marrying Angela very soon. And how can I bear it?

With a calm born of despair, she said, 'Good news, *signore*? That sounds exciting.'

'It will solve certain problems,' he said. 'But, all the same, you may not approve.'

The chicken was wonderful, but she might as well have been chewing sawdust.

She said carefully, 'It's really none of my business.'

'You are wrong, Lucia. It concerns you very closely.' He paused. 'Maddalena is coming back.' He observed her stunned expression, his mouth twisting. 'You were not expecting that, I think.'

'Well—no.' None of her tortuous imaginings had come up with that one, she thought, swallowing. 'How—how did you find her?'

'She found me. She came to the bank in a terrible state, distressed and crying, begging me to forgive her—to help her. It seems Moressi has been arrested for some other fraud, and is now in jail.' He spread his hands. 'She has worked for our family for a long time. She is not a criminal herself—just fatally weak where her nephew is concerned.' He paused. 'Although now she has learned, with great sadness, that she can be weak no longer.'

Lucy ate some salad. 'And of course she'll want to come back to the *casetta*.' She spoke her thought aloud. 'I'll need to move out.'

'Yes.' She was aware of his searching gaze, but took care not to meet it. 'So, you are free, Lucia. Free to go home at last—to get on with your life. Does that please you?'

'Well, naturally.' She put down her plate and fork. Her mouth was dry, her heart hammering. 'It—it's marvellous news. Although I shall miss Emilia and Marco, of course.'

She hesitated. 'What about the children? Will Maddelena be able to look after them as well as the house?'

'I think so. When she is not terrified out of her wits about Tommaso and what he will do next, she is very capable.' He paused. 'Anyway, it will not be for very long.'

Lucy said woodenly, 'Then it's all worked out perfectly.' She wanted to cry and howl, to beat the earth with her fists, and scream her misery at the uncaring sun.

But, more dangerously, at the same time she wanted to reach across the small space between them and touch his hand, feel the crispness of his dark hair under her fingers just once more, encounter the lean strength of his body under her questing hands.

Free to go, she thought with irony. What freedom will I ever know again?

'All for the best, indeed.' His tone was expressionless. 'And you, Lucia. What will you do?'

She shrugged. 'Get the next available flight back to Britain, naturally.' Her voice sounded light and rather brittle.

'Of course.' There was a silence. 'As I told you originally, Lucia, I shall meet all your expenses in this matter. But are you so keen to rush away? Would you not like to continue your vacation—to explore my Tuscany? You have seen and done so little...'

She thought, I've changed my life. I've discovered what love should be. I've broken my heart. What more could there possibly be?

Anguish gripped her by the throat, but she managed to speak normally. 'It's a kind thought, *signore*, but I have to go back—pick up the threads. And the sooner the better.'

He said quietly, 'You touched *il Porcellino*. So one day you will have to return to Firenze.'

She forced her stiff lips into a smile. 'I don't believe in superstition.' Or in fairy tales. Or in happy ever after, she added silently. She drank some wine, feeling it run down her throat like ice. 'And, anyway, this is the perfect place—the perfect way to say goodbye.' She held up her glass in mimicry of a toast. '*Salute.*'

Something flickered in the amber eyes as he lifted his glass in response.

'You are glad to be leaving?'

'Well...' Lucy studied minutely the bubbles in her wine '...all good things must come to an end.'

'You consider that your time here has been a good thing?'

'I think I've done a reasonable job.'

'That,' he said, 'is not what I asked.'

She said in a low voice, 'It hasn't always been easy.'

'No,' he said, and anger burned in his voice. 'It has been *il purgatorio*—the tortures of the damned '

Lucy bent her head. 'I'm sorry.'

'Why do you apologise when I alone am to blame? The entire situation was of my making.'

She said painfully, not looking at him, 'Not—all of it.'

'No.' The fine mouth twisted. 'You are right, of course. The wanting was—mutual, I think, and for that we must share the guilt.'

Her voice was husky. 'We—we shouldn't talk about guilt. Not on a day like this—when everything's so beautiful.'

'And you,' he said, 'the most beautiful of all. Ah, Lucia . . .'

She had not dared reach for him, but his fingers closed round hers instead, drawing her towards him with an insistence, a mastery that withstood any thought of denial. Words of negation—of self-preservation—drummed in her head, but she had no time to utter them. No time, nor any real inclination, she realised with her last coherent thought as she went into Giulio's arms.

His other hand possessively cradled her head as he bent from the dazzle of sunlight to kiss her mouth.

Her response was instant, incandescent, her lips trembling apart in welcome and surrender. Mouths locked, they drank from each other in the sweet delirium of their kiss.

Lucy was hardly aware of the actual moment when his weight bore her backwards down onto the rug. She already felt part of him, her entire being brought to vibrant life by the warmth of his body against hers.

The rush of the nearby water was echoed by the singing of her blood, by the moist heat of longing in her loins.

He kissed the line of her throat, his lips lingering erotically on the sensitive area below her ear. When he finally reached the delicate hollow at the base, he buried his face there for a moment, raggedly breathing in the scent of her skin.

His hands were shaking as they loosened the buttons on her shirt and drew it apart. The amber eyes were lambent, almost golden as he looked down at her.

He whispered, 'There has not been a moment of any day—of any night—when I have not thought of you—remembered you—wanted you—like this. Ah, *mia bella—mia carissima . . .*'

His mouth was reverent, almost worshipful as it moved on her skin. His palms cupped the roundness of her naked breasts, while his thumbs brushed her nipples with gentle sensuality, making her whole body twist beneath him in quivering delight.

When he took first one aroused, rosy peak and then the other into his mouth, an involuntary moan of pleasure tore from Lucy's throat. Her hips lifted towards him in mute entreaty, begging him to remove the last barrier. Longing for the ecstasy of his caress at the secret core of her womanhood, for the triumph of his maleness to be enclosed in her deep liquid flame.

She wanted to pleasure him—to satisfy him in undreamed-of ways. To be his woman, his lover, throughout some passionate eternity, and to die the little death of all lovers in his arms.

And felt him, instead, suddenly and unbelievably, draw back from her. Heard his voice, like a stranger's say, 'This is madness.'

'Giulio?' She knelt upright, her hands clinging to the front of his shirt, feeling the hurry of his heartbeat under her palm. 'What's wrong?'

His laugh was mirthless. 'Almost everything, I would say, *columbina*—wouldn't you?'

'You said you wanted me.' Pride no longer mattered, she realised numbly.

'Yes,' he said quietly. 'I want you—so badly that I was ready to forget honour—every other obligation—so that I might lose myself in you for a while. And I lose my own soul in consequence,' he added with sombre bitterness.

The golden radiance of the sun was shattering, fragmenting into shimmering droplets which stung her eyes and burned like acid on her skin. She shivered, forcing back the tears. Drawing the rags of her courage around her.

'Forgive me, Lucia.' He took her small, clenched fists and carried them to his lips. 'I should have stayed in Firenze.' He threw back his head and looked up at the sky, the muscles taut in his throat, his voice suddenly harsh. 'I should have known I could not trust myself.'

There was a silence, then he looked at her again, still kneeling rigidly in front of him, and his face and tone softened. 'Try not to hate me. Try to understand why I must be strong for us both, even now—at the moment of no return.'

'There's no such thing.' Somehow Lucy clambered to her feet, her fingers clumsy as she forced her shirt buttons back through their holes. 'There's always a way back.'

Unless you love someone as I love you—beyond pride, or honour, or even reason. Unless you're prepared to sacrifice them all for the beloved—as I would have done for you.

The unspoken words beat at her brain and scalded her heart. *Anything,* she thought with pain. *I would have done anything . . .*

She lifted her chin. 'Will you take me back to the villa, please? I—I want to pack.' And she saw him bend his head in silent acquiescence.

The return journey seemed endless. Giulio stared ahead of him, his face like a bronze mask, in a silence Lucy did not dare to break, even if she could have found the words to do so.

To her relief, he drove straight round to the *casetta*. As soon as the car stopped, she scrambled out, desperate to get away, to be alone when her self-control snapped.

But Giulio came after her, stopping her in the doorway, turning her to face him, his hands like iron on her shoulders. He said huskily, 'Don't hate me, *mia cara*, or I shall not be able to bear it. This is for the best. We must both believe that.'

'Yes.' Her smile felt as if it had been nailed there. 'All for the best.' She took a step backwards, away from him, holding out a determined hand. 'Goodbye, *signore*.'

'*Al diavolo!*' He almost spat the words. 'To hell with it. That is no way to part, Lucia. It must be like this.' And regardless of her stifled protest, he took her in his arms, and kissed her slowly and deeply on the mouth.

'*Addio.*' He held her for a moment, and she felt him trace the sign of the cross on her forehead. He said very quietly, 'Remember always—as I shall.'

Then he turned and walked away. Lucy stood very still, staring after him, listening to the subdued growl of the car engine as it powered into life, watching as he drove swiftly away, under the arch, leaving a faint haze of exhaust fumes in his wake, which would soon disappear also.

And she knew that she had never felt so alone in her life.

CHAPTER FOURTEEN

Lucy was halfway through her packing when she heard someone knocking at the door. When she went down, she was surprised to find the *contessa's* sour-faced maid waiting on the doorstep.

I must stop calling her that. Her name's Agnese, she thought guiltily, and tried a welcoming smile which was not reciprocated. In fact, the older woman looked grimmer than ever as she explained, in a few terse words of Italian, that Signora Rinaldi and the children had returned, and Lucy was wanted at the villa.

More goodbyes to be said, she acknowledged with an inward sigh and a polite word of thanks.

She found Fiammetta in the *salotto*, with Marco, who was playing with his car. Emilia, however, was nowhere to be seen.

Fiammetta was transformed, her face alight. 'Lucia—such wonderful news. Giulio was here, waiting for us, when we returned.'

'Yes, I know.' Lucy forced a smile. 'He—he told me, too—about Maddelena.'

'Maddalena?' Fiammetta echoed scornfully. 'Maddalena is nothing to this.' She raised rapturously clasped hands. 'Sergio is coming back. Giulio says he will be here tomorrow.'

'That's marvellous,' Lucy said, and meant it for all kinds of reasons. 'I'm really happy for you.'

'Oh, I cannot wait to see him. In the morning, I shall go to the beauty salon in Siena. And buy something new to wear.' Fiammetta plunged into a world of fabrics, colours and designers.

When she paused for breath, Lucy said mildly, 'I'll take the children down to the *casetta* to change for dinner. Is Emilia playing outside?'

'I left her in my room. She wished to dress up in some of my clothes.' Fiammetta's pretty brow creased. 'Blue, do you think, or perhaps a really deep yellow...?'

Lucy sighed, and went upstairs. She found Emilia parading up and down in a pink dress which trailed everywhere, a handbag dangling from her wrist.

'I am a *principessa*,' she announced.

Lucy dropped a curtsy. 'Then it's time Your Highness changed for tonight's state banquet.'

Emilia allowed herself one pout, but submitted with rare docility to being divested of the pink creation and taken back to the *casetta*.

Both children were in good spirits, sky-high over the news about their father. And Emilia was clearly relieved that Alison was making good progress, and soon to be discharged from the clinic.

'I miss her.' A small hand was slipped into Lucy's. 'Not that I do not like you, Lucia.'

'Yes.' Marco gave her a quick hug, too. 'Shall we ask Papà if you can come to the sea with us, Lucia?'

'That's sweet of you.' Lucy smiled at him. 'But I have to go back to England now. Maddalena's taking my place, you see.'

'Since I woke up this morning, everything has changed.' Emilia sounded slightly uncertain about this swift passage of events.

'That's life,' Lucy confirmed drily.

She would have to finish her packing in the morning, she decided, glancing at the half-full suitcase on her bed as she changed into a simple black shift which she'd selected from the garments still hanging in the wardrobe. Only one more meal to endure, she reminded herself, trying to cheer herself up—to alleviate the aching hollowness inside her which had nothing to do with hunger.

The walk up to the villa was lively enough, with a child attached to each hand, chattering nineteen to the dozen. But as soon as they entered the hall Lucy knew something was wrong.

Teresa was standing in the doorway to the kitchen, her face blank with dismay, while from the *salotto* the *contessa's* shrill voice could be heard ranting fortissimo, interspersed with Fiammetta's softer tones.

'*Cosa succede?*' Lucy asked. 'What's happening?'

Teresa lifted her shoulders in a shrug that mingled incomprehension with incredulity and vanished back into the kitchen.

Lucy found she was bracing herself as she pushed open the *salotto* door. Her instinct had not misled her.

'Ah.' Claudia Falcone turned like a tigress sighting her prey. 'The so-good, so-trusted Signorina Winters. Perhaps she can explain this mystery.'

'Mamma,' Fiammetta protested instantly. 'You have no right...'

'I have any right I choose. We know nothing of this girl, who appeared from nowhere so conveniently in this house. She has no references—no recommendation from anyone we know.'

'From Giulio,' Fiammetta ventured unhappily.

The *contessa* made a sweeping gesture of dismissal. 'That is another acquaintance which has never been explained to my satisfaction. Who knows what they have been to each other—or what this—this *puttana* may have read into it?'

Lucy's Italian might still be sketchy, but she knew what she'd just been called, and outraged colour stormed into her face.

She said in a choked voice, 'How dare you...?'

'Oh, do not play the innocent, *signorina*. Do you think we are all blind—that we have not seen the way you gaze at my stepson...?'

There was a small, stifled sound, and Lucy saw that tears were running down Emilia's cheeks.

'*Cara.*' She went down on one knee beside the child, as Marco too burst into noisy sobs.

'Mamma!' This time Fiammetta's voice held a note of steel. 'That is enough.' She went to the door and called to Teresa, who appeared with discreet promptness and whisked both children away.

'Lucia, we have a problem. Something bad has happened, and we are all a little upset. The ruby—the Falcone ring—has vanished from my mother's bedroom. We have searched everywhere but found no trace of it.' She paused in obvious distress. 'You understand we must ask, difficult though it is, if you have seen it.'

There was a brief, loaded silence, then Fiammetta went on almost desperately, 'You see, Lucia, you were here alone today. Both Angela and Philip left for the day while my mother was still in her room, and neither of them has returned yet.' There was another pause. 'Perhaps you saw someone—a stranger—who could have entered the villa—'

'Fiammetta, you are a fool,' the *contessa* broke in impatiently. 'There was no *stranger*.' She spat the word. 'The girl already pries where she has no business. Agnese saw her coming out of my room a week ago. And today Giulio tells her that Maddalena is returning, and that her time here is at an end, so she decides she will award herself a bonus for her dubious services. No more discussion—let us call the police.'

Lucy stared at her. She said slowly, 'You think I stole the Falcone ring? You must be mad.'

'No. It is you that is mad—crazy because my stepson is to be married and no longer wants you. And you think to take revenge by taking the family ring—the symbol of his engagement to my niece.'

Lucy turned to Fiammetta. 'Signora Rinaldi, surely you don't think...?'

'I do not know what to think.' Fiammetta's face was as miserable as sin. 'But we have searched here, and now

Mamma insists we must look in the *casetta*. You do not object, I hope.'

'Of course not—' Lucy began, and halted, beset by a sudden feeling of trepidation. Emilia, she thought slowly, remembering the sudden, unexpected outburst of tears. Emilia playing upstairs alone—being a *principessa*. Surely—*surely* after Lucy's warning she hadn't taken the ring again. She couldn't have done. Or could she...?

'Signorina Winters seems to be having second thoughts.' The *contessa's* voice sounded almost triumphant.

'No,' Lucy denied swiftly. 'I'm quite prepared to have my things searched.'

As long as it ends there, she thought. As long as they don't go into the children's rooms. If Emilia has taken it, I'll get it back and return it somehow. Make them think they didn't search thoroughly enough.

'And will you also explain why you were in my room the other day?'

Lucy paused. 'I was playing hide-and-seek with the children.'

'Ah.' The *contessa's* smile was thin. 'And today, once more, we will—seek what you have hidden.'

'Mamma.' Fiammetta sounded desperate. 'You must not say these things. The ring may simply be lost...'

'Nonsense,' the *contessa* said with contempt. 'It has been stolen, and by this girl—this *sciattona*. We will search the *casetta* now.'

'May I ask a question?' Lucy kept her voice even. 'How did you know Count Falcone has spoken to me— about leaving?'

'Agnese saw you together—at the *casetta*.' Claudia Falcone's tone held jeering malice. 'Since you have been here, *signorina*, she has maintained a watchful eye—on my instructions.'

Lucy remembered that last passionate kiss, and felt as if she'd been dipped in slime.

She said quietly, 'I see.'

But at least I wasn't just being paranoid when I thought someone was spying on me, she thought wearily, recalling her unease that day beside the pool.

Agnese was waiting to accompany them back to the *casetta*. So the *contessa* wasn't going to soil her hands with the actual search, Lucy realised angrily, encountering her sly, knowing look.

She turned to Fiammetta. 'Is this really necessary?'

'My mother wishes it, Lucia—I am sorry...'

'Not half as sorry as I am,' Lucy said grimly, and set off.

Claudia Falcone didn't waste a second in the living room. Agnese following, she went straight up to Lucy's bedroom. She pointed to the open case on the bed. 'Look there.'

As if in a dream, Lucy watched Agnese pick up her yellow dress and shake out the folds. A small tissue-wrapped bundle fell to the floor, and the *contessa* pounced on it with a cry of triumph. The Falcone ring gleamed like blood in her hand.

The dress I wore to Firenze, Lucy thought numbly. Odd that Emilia should have chosen that one as a hiding place. But at least she had the sense not to conceal it in her own things.

'Not even a clever thief, *signorina*.' Claudia Falcone replaced the ring gloatingly on her finger, and looked at Fiammetta. 'Now we will call the police.'

'No.' Fiammetta sounded more firm than Lucy had ever heard her. 'I will not permit it. You have the ring, Mamma, so be content. Lucia is leaving tomorrow, and Giulio—believe me—would not wish a scandal.' There was pain in the glance she directed at Lucy, and reproach. 'You have some explanation, Lucia?'

Yes, thought Lucy, but not one I can ever make. Emilia's only a child. She doesn't understand that her actions can have consequences—and this would be a hard way to teach her. In fact, it would probably be disastrous. And what real purpose would it serve—as I'm going anyway? As I'll never have to see any of these people again.

Lifting her chin, she said quietly, 'I cannot account, *signora*, for the ring being in my case. I can only say I did not put it there.'

'Then there is no more to be said.' Fiammetta's sigh rose from the soles of her elegant shoes. 'I will arrange for a meal to be served to you here this evening, and tomorrow Franco will drive you to Montiverno, where you can catch a bus to Pisa. You will understand that I do not wish you to have any further contact with my children. They can sleep at the villa tonight.'

After the shocks and insults of the past half-hour, it was strange how that hurt the most...

Moving like an automaton, Lucy completed her packing. From what Fiammetta had said, it was evident that she was going to be dumped, and left to make her own way home as best she could. She counted her money, then counted it again, doing rapid sums in her head and deriving no comfort from her calculations. If she couldn't change the return portion of her air ticket to an earlier flight, she would be in real trouble.

When an unhappy Teresa brought her supper tray, she steeled herself to give her a note for Philip.

The evening dragged endlessly past, and she was just on the point of giving him up altogether and going to bed when he appeared reluctantly at the door.

'You've got a damned cheek, sending for me,' was his greeting. 'They'll probably think we're in it together.'

Lucy gasped. 'You can't possibly believe I stole the ring.'

'Well, someone did,' he returned unarguably. 'Although Angela thinks it was an act of spite rather than a theft, because you wanted Giulio Falcone for yourself.'

'I'm sure it's the twisted way she would think,' Lucy said icily. 'But her opinions don't interest me. The thing is—' she took a deep breath '—I need to borrow some money to get me back to Britain.'

'And you want me to give it to you? When you've done your best to freeze me out for the past week?'

'A temporary loan, that's all.' Lucy swallowed. 'Philip, believe me, I wouldn't ask if I wasn't desperate. And I'll repay you as soon as I get back.'

'Or you could repay me now—in kind.' His tone was calculating. 'What do you say, Luce? A roll in the sack for old times' sake?'

His hand on her shoulder, and then sliding down insinuatingly towards her breast, made her realise, with shock, that he wasn't joking.

She stepped backwards. She said between her teeth, 'On second thoughts, I'd rather walk home.'

'Fine.' His voice was savage. 'You're just not very lucky, are you, Luce? Two men in your life, and you've lost them both to Angela. No wonder she's laughing all over her face.'

The carafe of wine was still on her untouched supper tray. Lucy said crisply, 'Then let's give her another giggle,' and threw it at him.

For a moment, he stood frozen, the ruby liquid dripping off his nose and chin, soaking into his expensive silk shirt. Then he said, 'Bitch!' with venomous clarity, and walked out with as much dignity as he could muster.

Franco arrived apologetically at the door almost as soon as it was daylight. It was clear that the family could not wait to get her off the premises, Lucy thought, biting her lip, as her luggage was loaded into the car. It was an awkward, embarrassing journey, and she was glad when they reached Montiverno.

She was surprised to find her hand shaken warmly in parting. *'Ti credo, signorina,'* Franco told her. 'I believe you, and Teresa also.'

There were tears in her eyes as he drove away. And she could have cried all over again when she worked out how long she was going to wait for the bus to Pisa. Partly because she was starving and partly to fill the time she bought herself a cup of coffee and a brioche at the café near the bus stop, then settled herself on a bench to wait.

She tried to read, but couldn't concentrate. Her head was whirling with disconnected thoughts, most of them unhappy. She hated leaving Tuscany under a cloud, even though it was no fault of hers. The knowledge that Angela and the *contessa* were gloating over her downfall was agonising, and so was the loss of Fiammetta's good opinion. Above all, however, two people dominated her reverie: Emilia, her small face pinched and wan, and Giulio.

Nausea twisted in her stomach as she tried to imagine what he would be told—what he would think. How she would inevitably be condemned unheard.

Yet he was the only one who would understand what Emilia had done—and why. The only one who would keep the information to himself, and forgive the child. As well as give the help she so badly needed.

She heard the hiss of brakes, and saw a bus pulling up at the stop, its destination board showing 'Firenze'.

Lucy got to her feet, aware of a trembling in the pit of her stomach. I have to tell him, she thought. For Emilia's sake, he has to know, so that he can protect her. Or it will happen all over again, and his stepmother will have her put in some ghastly institution, where she'll be marked for life.

It was a quick and straightforward journey, but Lucy was chafing with impatience just the same by the time they arrived in Florence. The bus stopped near the train station, so Lucy checked her case and bags into the left-luggage facility, then called into the nearby tourist office for directions to the Falcone bank.

It was a relatively new building in an anonymous street off the Piazza della Repubblica, and Lucy found herself having to negotiate stringent security precautions at its imposing glass entrance.

Her insistence that she needed a personal interview with Count Giulio Falcone was received politely but sceptically. Eventually, she was confronted by a middle-aged secretary who explained with remote civility that Count Falcone was not available.

Lucy's hands twisted together. 'Then if you could just give him a message...'

'I am sorry, *signorina*. He will not be here for the rest of the day. He was called away earlier on urgent family business.'

And that, Lucy thought wretchedly, could mean anything.

Well, I tried, she thought, trying to comfort herself as she made her way back to the station, only to find that she had just missed a connection to Pisa, and had an hour to wait.

But what real hurry was there anyway? she asked herself. She walked slowly out of the station and back into the city. Giulio's city. Wanting to see it through his eyes. Wishing she could know it as he did. Retracing the steps of the route she had followed during their brief time there together. It was, after all, her last chance.

In the little street near the Duomo, Giovanni's restaurant was already bustling, getting ready for the day. Lucy wished she could have eaten there, but the need to conserve her money in case of problems at the airport seemed more important, she conceded with a sigh, before turning into the long street leading down to the Piazza della Signoria.

In the adjoining Mercato Nuovo, Il Porcellino, the bronze wild boar, sat grinning amiably.

I did return, Lucy told him under her breath, but not in the way I wanted. And I won't be coming back. She lifted a hand and stroked the gleaming snout in final farewell.

* * *

Pisa lay baked in mid-afternoon sun when Lucy finally arrived at Galileo Galilei airport. She loaded her bags onto a trolley, and set off for the terminal building, mentally rehearsing what she'd have to say.

As the doors slid apart to admit her, he was the first—the only one—she saw.

He was standing directly in front of her, hands on hips, his face tired and serious, the golden gleam of laughter and life gone from his amber eyes. It occurred to her as she hesitated, the chatter of voices, the buzz of movement fading into obscurity, that she would give a year of her life to see him smile again.

He stepped forward and put a hand on the trolley, halting its progress. 'So,' he said quietly. 'You are here at last.'

Lucy's heart performed a peculiar kind of somersault. She said huskily, 'Are you having me arrested? Or just making sure I leave the country?'

'Neither of those things, Lucia. You should know better than that.'

She wasn't sure of anything any more. But one thing she had to make clear.

She threw back her head. 'Giulio—I swear to you I didn't do it—I didn't take the ring.' She paused. 'But I'm afraid I know who did.'

'I do too,' he said, the weary lines beside his mouth deepening. 'And I am more sorry than I can say.'

She wanted to take his head in her hands and kiss away the strain and unhappiness. She said, 'Don't be too hard on her—please. She's unhappy and confused—and I think she was doing it for you.'

'You can say that?' he asked harshly. 'If she'd had her way you would have been in a police cell by now.'

Lucy shivered. 'She doesn't think things through. I'm sure she never intended...'

'You are wrong, Lucia. She wished to destroy you. Sergio and I have had to listen to it all—to every poisonous, twisted thought she has ever had.' He drew a harsh breath. 'It was—vile.'

Lucy moved sharply in negation. 'Darling—don't. She's only a child. She doesn't realise...'

'A child?' His brows lifted. 'I doubt that Claudia was ever a child.'

'*Claudia?*' Lucy almost screamed the name. 'But she didn't steal the ring.'

'*Sì.*' Giulio bent his head. 'She gave it to her witch of a maid to put among your things. Surely you must have known?'

She said numbly. 'No. I—I thought it was Emilia.'

'Emilia?' Giulio echoed. 'But what possible reason...?'

Lucy stared up at him. 'She'd heard you arguing with your stepmother about it and wanted to help. She took it once before—so that she could return it to you. I knew what Contessa Falcone would make of it if she found out, so I put it back. Only Agnese saw me, it seems.'

'So that was it,' Giulio said grimly. 'She has been spying on you from the beginning, and saw me kiss you yesterday. When she reported back to Claudia, they hatched this plot to get rid of you, hoping that you would be back in England in disgrace before I heard of it.'

'It's unbelievable.'

'Not if you know Claudia.' Giulio sighed, then glanced around, regaining authority as he registered the curious glances being directed at them.

'We cannot stay here,' he said. 'We'll take your luggage to the car, and find somewhere to talk in private.'

Lucy hung back, her face troubled. 'I've got to see about my ticket. I—I have to leave—to go back. I just needed you to know that I wasn't a thief.'

'*Idiota.*' His voice was very tender. 'Little fool. Little dove. Did you really think I would let you go?'

'You can't keep me here,' Lucy protested as he began to steer the trolley out of the terminal building. 'You have no right—not when you're going to marry Angela.'

'Let us be clear.' He didn't even pause. 'I am not marrying Angela now, or at any future time. I do not love Angela, and I never have. As she and Claudia are now finally aware,' he added with chill emphasis.

'You don't want her?' Lucy's voice shook.

He said gently, 'I love you, Lucia, and as soon as we have some privacy I shall ask you to be my wife. But not, I think, standing in the middle of a car park.'

Lucy, rendered unexpectedly dumb, followed him meekly to the car.

'So, here we are,' he said as he slid into the driver's seat beside her. 'Back where it all began.' He reached into the inside pocket of his jacket and brought out the Falcone ring. 'Give me your hand, *carissima*.'

She obeyed, and he put the glowing ruby on her finger.

'Now,' he said softly. 'Now, my love, my wife, do you believe me?' And he kissed her deeply and tenderly, and then with a mounting passion that sent her head and her heart reeling.

When she was allowed to speak, Lucy said breathlessly, 'But you sent me away. You said it would be dishonourable for you to—touch me. That you had other commitments—obligations.'

'Not I, *mia bella*, you, or so I thought. I believed you were still in love with your worthless Philip. I found his photograph torn up in your room that first day at the villa, and recognised him as the new man in Angela's life.'

'But how could you? You'd never met him, surely?'

Giulio shrugged. 'Angela is going to be a rich woman,' he said drily. 'Her father is naturally cautious about any man she dates—has private enquiries made about his background. And I see the information as a security precaution, because of the connection between our families. I was not impressed with what I read,' he added levelly.

He paused. 'When I went to Lussione and questioned your friends, they confirmed that Philip had left you for another woman, and that you were devastated—heart-broken. The last thing I bargained for was Angela's arrival with this Philip.

'I could think of nothing but how hurt you were going to be, and of how much I wanted to protect you from that hurt. That was when I knew I felt more for you than a passing attraction. When I knew I had fallen in love with you the first moment that you trembled in my arms.'

The beginnings of a smile curved Lucy's mouth. 'I think that's when it began for me too—*caro* Giulio.'

He lifted the hand that wore his ring to his lips. 'What fools we have been. The time we have wasted.' He sighed. 'But, you see, I'd made up my mind that if Philip—' he pronounced the name with disdain '—was the man you truly wanted I would not stand in your way, however much I wanted you for myself.'

His mouth hardened. 'It wasn't such a problem. I know Angela only too well—know how easily she can be diverted. So I—quite cynically, I confess—provided the appropriate diversion.'

'But how could you have thought I still wanted Philip?' The colour rose in Lucy's face. 'When you saw how I—reacted to you—responded to you.'

He stroked her flushed cheek with a gentle hand. 'Sex is a great deceiver, Lucia. I tried so hard to tell myself you belonged to someone else. That I had no right to confuse you—to seduce you away from your real love.'

He shook his head. 'I tried desperately, too, to hold back from you—and each time I failed I despised myself more. That's why I went to Firenze. Because I could no longer trust myself to be near you.'

'But I never gave Philip any encouragement,' Lucy protested. 'In fact I realised almost as soon as he went that our relationship had been going nowhere, and that he'd done us both a favour by pulling out. I admit it was a shock when he first left, but my pride was hurt far more than my heart.'

'But the girl—Nina—was so sure. She said you were a one-man woman. That you'd been close to a breakdown over him.'

Lucy bit her lip. 'Nina and I work for the same company but we've never been close friends, and I've never confided in her. I think she had her own agenda in this.'

Giulio groaned. 'I should have asked you what your feelings were—but I did not dare.'

Lucy touched the crimson fire of the Falcone ring with a gentle hand. 'Presumably something happened to change your mind?'

'Ah, yes.' The familiar gleam of laughter had returned to the amber eyes. 'Fiammetta told me something about him being drenched in wine last night. That did not seem like a token of love, *columbina*. Coupled with the fact that he had allowed you to leave alone, his eagerness to dissociate himself from the supposed theft— and certain ill-judged remarks about your frigidity,' he added with something like a snarl. 'He has Sergio to thank that I did not break his jaw. But when I left he and Angela were engaged in mutual recriminations, so I suppose that is punishment enough.'

Her mouth trembled into a smile. 'Almost certainly.' She paused. 'But how did you find out about Claudia?'

'We have Sergio to thank. He arrived at the villa early this morning, just after your departure, and found the place in uproar. It did not take him long to realise that Emilia was troubled. She'd overheard part of a conversation between Agnese and Claudia, and although she did not completely understand it she told Sergio enough to make him suspicious. He thought it best to send for me, and between us we got the truth from Agnese, and eventually Claudia herself,' he explained grimly.

'I ordered her to pack her things and leave immediately. But not before I had told her that all her plotting had failed, and that I would never willingly see her again. Then I left poor Sergio to sort out the mess and came to Pisa to find you. I've been here most of the day.'

Lucy sighed. 'And I was in Firenze looking for you. I couldn't bear to leave without seeing you again.'

'Oh, you would have seen me again,' he told her softly. 'Even if you had gone with Philip, I would have followed—tried to make you change your mind. You see, *cara*, I cannot live without you.'

'Nor I without you.' Lucy looked at him from under her lashes, suddenly shy. 'But it's all happened so fast...'

'It was the same with my mother and father,' he said gently, his mouth curving in tender reminiscence. 'One look—one smile—and they were lost.' He smoothed a strand of Lucy's hair back from her forehead. 'Now, *columbina*, do you believe in the force of destiny?'

'I think I must,' she said softly.

Giulio nodded. 'By the time we get back to the villa, everyone will have gone. Sergio is taking his own family away, so you will meet him later—when Fiammetta is less distraught,' he added with a small grimace. 'So you and I, *mia bella*, will have some time to ourselves at last to make plans for our marriage.'

He paused. 'But now you have something to tell me, I think.'

'Have I?' Lucy frowned. 'We seem to have covered everything.'

'Not quite.' The amber gaze was steadfast, intent on her face, brilliant with tenderness and need. 'You have never yet, Lucia *mia*, told me that you love me.'

Lucy put her arms round his neck and drew him towards her.

'I think,' she whispered as her lips touched his, 'that I shall spend the rest of my life doing exactly that, *mi amore*.'

Take 4 bestselling love stories FREE

Plus get a FREE surprise gift!

Special Limited-time Offer

Mail to Harlequin Reader Service®

3010 Walden Avenue
P.O. Box 1867
Buffalo, N.Y. 14240-1867

YES! Please send me 4 free Harlequin Presents® novels and my free surprise gift. Then send me 6 brand-new novels every month, which I will receive months before they appear in bookstores. Bill me at the low price of $3.12 each plus 25¢ delivery and applicable sales tax, if any*. That's the complete price and a savings of over 10% off the cover prices—quite a bargain! I understand that accepting the books and gift places me under no obligation ever to buy any books. I can always return a shipment and cancel at any time. Even if I never buy another book from Harlequin, the 4 free books and the surprise gift are mine to keep forever.

106 HEN CE65

Name	(PLEASE PRINT)
Address	Apt. No.
City	State
	Zip

This offer is limited to one order per household and not valid to present Harlequin Presents® subscribers. *Terms and prices are subject to change without notice. Sales tax applicable in N.Y.

UPRES-696 ©1990 Harlequin Enterprises Limited

Presents Extravaganza
25 YEARS!

With the purchase of two Harlequin Presents® books, you can send in for a FREE Silvertone Book Pendant. Retail value $19.95. It's our gift to you!

FREE SILVERTONE BOOK PENDANT

On the official proof-of-purchase coupon below, fill in your name, address and zip or postal code, and send it, plus $1.50 U.S./ $2.50 CAN. for postage and handling, (check or money order—please do not send cash), to Harlequin books: In the U.S.: 3010 Walden Avenue, P.O. Box 9077, Buffalo, N.Y. 14269-9077; In Canada: P.O. Box 609, Fort Erie, Ontario L2A 5X3. Please allow 4-6 weeks for delivery. Order your Silvertone Book Pendant now! Quantities are limited. Offer for the FREE Silvertone Book Pendant expires December 31, 1998.

Coming Next Month

HARLEQUIN PRESENTS®

THE BEST HAS JUST GOTTEN BETTER!

#1965 FANTASY FOR TWO Penny Jordan
Mollie Barnes and Alex Villiers seemed to have nothing in common. So why had she confessed her secret fantasy to him? And why was it they couldn't seem to keep away from each other?

#1966 THE DIAMOND BRIDE Carole Mortimer
(Nanny Wanted!)
Annie adored being Jessica Diamond's nanny, but her relationship with Jessica's father was complicated! Rufus had the power to make her laugh and cry—he also wanted to make love to her! But Jessica had to come first....

#1967 RENDEZVOUS WITH REVENGE Miranda Lee
When Abby's boss, Ethan Grant, asked her to pose as his lover at the conference, she knew that to him she was probably just an expensive plaything. In fact, she turned out to be a pawn in his game of revenge!

#1968 THE GROOM SAID MAYBE! Sandra Marton
(The Wedding of the Year)
It all began when Stephanie and David were seated next to each other at a wedding. Stephanie needed a lawyer, and David was one of the best, so she told him she needed money. Then David confessed he needed a fiancée....

#1969 LONG-DISTANCE MARRIAGE Sharon Kendrick
Alessandra and Cameron married in haste, believing that they could combine two careers in two different cities. But with the pressure came problems, particularly when he suggested that she leave work to have his baby....

#1970 LOVERS' LIES Daphne Clair
Joshua didn't recognize Felicia, but his obvious attraction to her gave her the means to exact revenge for his betrayal of her stepsister years ago. The problem was, Felicia herself was not immune to his charms....